THE PUPPET MASTER

An MSCE Investigation

David A. Xavier

Order this book online at www.trafford.com
or email orders@trafford.com

Most Trafford titles are also available at major online book retailers.

Printed in the United States of America.

ISBN: 978-1-4907-4419-3 (sc)
ISBN: 978-1-4907-4420-9 (hc)
ISBN: 978-1-4907-4421-6 (e)

Library of Congress Control Number: 2014914348

Trafford rev. 02/02/2015

 www.trafford.com

North America & international
toll-free: 1 888 232 4444 (USA & Canada)
fax: 812 355 4082

A Dragon Literature production

www.dragonliterature.com

Acknowledgements

This book was initially written for the 2012 NaNoWriMo - National Novel Writer's Month, to the uninitiated. I made lots of friends during that month, many of whom I have remained in touch with since. I made even more friends the following year, in 2013's NaNoWriMo, and the constant support they have provided has helped me to create this work.

Special thanks to Catherine Quirk, my editor and best friend. Thanks to you, I learned the faith in myself that I needed to see this process through. This one is for you.

1

It was with a strange sense of calm that Ben Wattler closed the door behind him, and began what would be the final journey home of his life.

Everything seemed better now. It was astonishing how quickly troubles that had been eating him up for so many years seemed to have become ridiculous, understandable or solvable. He got into his car and drove with the new-found strength of self-belief. He could turn things around. He could put his life back on track if he just took a moment to understand each situation and make sure that he spoke out when he had to.

He took a little time going home. His BMW was a nice car, and it deserved to be put through its paces now and then, so he took a couple of backstreets and country lanes, allowing himself to gun the engine and speed a little.

He knew how to drive well, and therefore he used the open road for what it should be for - enjoyment and appreciation of his surroundings. Wheat, rape seed, berries, apples, whatever they were - he did not know and did not care: they were never so pretty as when they were obscured in the water-stain effect of motion blur. Different aromas assailed his senses as he flashed by fields, and the wind roared past him, whiting out all sound other than the engine's roar.

His phone rang. He closed the window, blotting out much of the noise and most of the scent, and depressed a button next to his dashboard. He said hello into the empty car.

"Ben, hello. Are you home yet?"

"No, I'm five minutes out."

"Good. When you get there, remember what we spoke about. You can sort this out, and it's really not as complicated as you have been making it out to be. Trust yourself, think about things before you say them, and just remember that as long as she fully appreciates how much you need to be heard, you won't have a problem. Take your cue from what's around, or from whatever she is doing. Lead into it naturally. If you haven't decided what she's going to say, you won't be as surprised when it's something you don't expect. It will be over before you know it."

Ben nodded. "You're right. I should have known that it would be simpler than I thought. Thank you. Listen, it has been too long. How about a drink some time, maybe dinner? That house of yours is a little pokey. No offence. We have a heated conservatory with a beautiful view. Maybe we can speak again once things are better, and you can visit."

"Sure. Like old times. Right."

Ben missed the sarcasm in the voice. "Great. I'll give you a call. Thanks again."

Ben hung up. Another button press and his window hummed back down into the door, letting in the crisp, cool air. It was one of those strange English April days. He found the bite in the wind bracing, but not unpleasant against the warmth of the sun.

He slowed down as he came towards the town's outskirts. No sense in spoiling a good day with a speeding fine. It was not far to his house now. He automatically began to run through what to say in his head, but then slapped the steering wheel with one hand.

"No," he said. "I will not pre-plan. I will allow this to unfold naturally. I will simply trust in my own ability to say what needs to be said, and in Chrissy's understanding."

The pep-talk worked. He laughed in surprise and adjusted his position in the seat, moving to sit up a little straighter. To his surprise, he even felt his mouth curl into the beginnings of a smile. Maybe he really could do this.

He did not even feel the expected fear of confrontation as he walked up to his front door a couple of moments later and slid the key into the lock.

"Hey, Chris? Chrissy? I'm home." He cocked his head, but did not hear a reply. He walked in through the hall and put his head into the living room. The crystal decanters were out on the table with a polishing cloth, but the room was empty. The dining room was equally quiet. He noted that the silver was sitting there as a reminder for him to set the table before dinner tonight.

Entering the kitchen, Ben heard a thump from the floor above - their bedroom. He called out again, but there was still no reply. He threw his jacket over the back of a chair and straightened it under the island counter in the centre of the kitchen. Then he spotted the knife block and absently picked out the carving knife. He tried the edge with his thumb and frowned. It was too blunt for efficient carving. He would have to sharpen it before he carved that night.

He turned back to the hall and jogged up the stairs, taking them two at a time. If Chrissy was not busy, there might be a chance to get this all sorted now before they had to start preparing for dinner. He walked to the bedroom and stopped for a moment in the doorway.

There were few things that would stop Ben Wattler in his tracks, but his wife's almost naked form was one of them. She stood with her back to him clad only in a white bra and thong combination that he loved. She held up two dresses, both red.

"Benny, which do you think?" she asked, not turning.

Ben could not see the difference, other than a slightly different shape around the neck. "I don't know. Babe, can we talk?"

"Sure. Talk and think. We need to think as well as talk."

Ben walked into the room so that he was standing behind her and tried to look interested in the dresses as she stood in front of her floor-length mirror.

"How was Joseph?"

The question threw him for a moment. Then he remembered he had told her he was seeing Joseph that morning.

"What? Oh, yes, he was fine. He had to leave. Something about the stag party tonight."

He hoped that would carry. Neville was getting married in three days, and Ben had been invited to his stag do, but Chrissy had overruled it. The soon-to-be-retiring president of the school committee was coming to dinner, and she wanted his job or something like that.

"That's all? You two usually go on for hours."

"Well, we didn't. Look, can we talk seriously for a moment? You need to listen to me. You never listen to me." He cursed inwardly. He was not thinking about what he needed to say, and not having prepared any kind of script was new and uncomfortable.

She turned then. There was a look of fury in her face, and she opened her mouth to yell, but then closed it and looked at him oddly.

"Why do you have that knife in your hand?"

Ben looked down and saw that he still held the carving knife. He stared at it for a minute and then blinked and looked back at Chrissy.

He blinked again.

As his eyes reopened, he pulled back in surprise, as Chrissy's face was suddenly a finger's length away from him. Her mouth was open and her eyes wide, and he became painfully aware that she was screaming. He looked down and saw blood pouring from her shoulders, neck and chest. Her white bra was stained red, and she had dropped the two dresses. She appeared to be trying to reach for him, but her arms were slick with blood and she could not seem to move them.

He threw his hands out to catch her as she staggered, but something stopped him and he slid slightly towards his left. He looked down at his right hand to see that it was still clutching the carving knife, which he had just pushed into Chrissy's stomach.

He let go and she crumpled to the floor with the sound of a heavy suitcase being dropped, but somehow stickier. He stepped back, breathing fast, and then started to cry out. He stumbled into the bed and then fell off it in his rush to get away. He pushed himself into the corner of the room and bellowed in fear and horror.

2

"I should not have climbed out of bed this morning," I muttered, even as I drove into Stapely Drive and turned off my car's siren so that only the blue lights on the roof continued flashing. Somehow, I just knew that today was not going to be an easy day. I pulled up behind the first response car and turned off the engine.

I looked at the young face of the man sitting in the passenger seat. He looked nervous.

"Come on Carrey," I said. "Let's go pay the dead people a visit."

Out of the corner of my eye, I saw Detective Constable Carrey swallow and take a breath before reaching for the handle of his door. Then I was out and walking towards the crime scene. As I reached the drive of number 72, three things struck me as odd.

Firstly, a racing green BMW M6 sat on the driveway with its driver's side door open, the window down, and the engine still idling. Secondly, the front door to the house was partially open, and the keys were still in the lock, which meant most likely that the first responder had found it that way. Thirdly, Police Constable Rickard was voiding the contents of his stomach rather violently into the flower bed by the front window of the property.

PC Morley stood guard by the front door, wrinkling his nose and wincing in Rickard's direction. As I approached he turned to me and nodded a greeting.

"Sarge," he said. "This is a messy one, sir."

"Are you referring to Rickard here, or the crime scene, Morley?"

He chuckled, and managed a weak smile. "Both, I think, sir. Murder-suicide upstairs in the bedroom and, well, not a pretty sight."

"Thank you, Morley," I said. "Who else is here?"

"Cartwright is upstairs with Norton, and everyone is on their way."

"Okay, Morley." I nodded my appreciation to the constable and turned to look at the apprehensive man beside me. "Right, lad, let's go."

Carrey passed me, looking slightly pale. I followed him into the house and, as I did, I thought I saw Morley's lips twitch into a grin for a moment. I let it slide and hurried after Carrey as Rickard started retching again.

The house was posh, there was no doubt about that. Five doors led off the main hall. One went into the front living room, one to the kitchen and one clearly opened into the garage. The other two were at the end of the hall and I ignored them for now. Carrey was walking back towards them, but I tapped his shoulder and beckoned him upstairs after me.

Four more rooms fed off the second-floor corridor, with another set of stairs going up to yet another level. Sergeant Cartwright stood outside one door, which was half open, and greeted us as we got to the top of the steps.

"Soames, Carrey."

"Cartwright." We nodded to each other, but I ground my teeth a little as I acknowledged him. I had a great deal of professional respect for Sergeant Cartwright's work. He was a good police officer. However, I did not have time for some of his personal prejudices. The half-sneer in his voice as he said Carrey's name annoyed me.

I moved to the doorway of the room and looked in. I registered that PC Norton was there already and then I saw red, and a lot of it. Whatever had happened here was violent and brutal.

"Norton," I said.

"Sergeant. Detective." He did not look directly at us as he replied, but continued scanning the scene. His voice was stilted and he spoke only absently in the overly formal attitude he only ever seemed to adopt at a crime scene. The expression in his eyes was almost feral, but I knew it well. I may not have been friends with Norton, but I'd worked a few cases with him and, unlike Cartwright, he had earned my respect as a person as well as a police officer.

I heard a gagging sound over my shoulder. Carrey was leaning over to look in and had turned rather puce.

"Outside, if you must," I said to him.

Carrey pursed his lips, clearly not wanting to show himself up, but then turned and ran back downstairs. Cartwright laughed, an unpleasant bark of sound. I glared at him and he stopped, though he made no attempt to wipe the smirk from his face.

"Not a pleasant induction for Detective Carrey." I turned to see Norton looking sympathetic and shot him a smile.

"No, I am afraid not."

"Still, new blood must be tested eventually." He winced. "Maybe not the best turn of phrase."

Norton turned back, and shook his head at something that was obscured by the bed from where I stood. I turned instead to the body lying in front of the mirror. Undergarments said this was a woman, as did the long blonde hair. Both were stained with red which also covered her entire body. Scratches decorated her face, body and arms, and her facial features were obscured by gashes and blood. Some cuts looked deep, the most obvious of which was to her upper abdomen from which protruded what looked like a large kitchen knife.

Streaks of red, like macabre decorations, had dripped down the mirror and the pale blue wardrobes that surrounded it. The carpeted floor around the body was soaked in blood and splashes surrounded the stain.

"Okay, Sniffer, what have you got?" I asked.

Norton turned to me. "It seems rather cut and dried," he said, and then winced again. "Not my day. Anyway, seems like a husband and wife. He killed her and then came to his senses, snapped, and killed himself. We still need ID to confirm that they are who we think. I'm going to check for forced entry though. Just to make sure."

I opened my mouth to ask him why if it was such an obvious case, but he was past me and hurrying down the stairs before I could. Norton was a queer one. We in the Criminal Investigation Department called him Sniffer, though it was not an entirely accurate nickname. He had exceptionally sharp eyes and would often look around a crime scene and see something the rest of the force might miss. Still, he did seem to be part-sniffer dog at times.

I liked to think that the CID were as good as him, but he had seen something in a rape case I had handled six months before that indicated a third person present. He had been partnered with Carrey, and it had been that case that had elevated Carrey himself to CID. I did not understand the politics behind it, but Norton did not seem to mind.

I moved further into the bedroom to look at the other side of the bed. I had not taken two paces when I saw the husband's body behind it. I walked round gingerly, avoiding the bloodstains. The man's body was slumped into the corner of the room and surrounded by another pool of blood. Long slashes stretched from the base of each of his wrists to a point fully halfway to his elbows. A stiletto-heeled shoe lay next to him, caked in blood, and I almost gagged as I realised that this was most likely his suicide weapon.

That was not the most disturbing thing, though. I looked up at what I had assumed from a distance was just another blood spatter on the wall and saw that it was writing. I took another couple of steps towards it so that I could see more clearly and realised that someone had written 'sorry' in blood dozens of times above the dead man.

3

"Who called it in, Cartwright?" I asked when I exited the bedroom.

"Old lady two doors down." He jerked his finger towards the wall of the Wattlers' bedroom. "She was taking her rubbish out and saw the car door had been left open, and then heard the screams." He passed me a piece of paper. "Occupants' identities. Just found them."

I headed back out of the house and looked in the direction Cartwright had indicated. A lady who looked to be in her seventies, wearing age-worn clothing, was talking to a police constable I did not recognise. Crime scene tape was being put up now, four new police cars dotted the road outside the house, and I could see that both ends of the road were now blocked off by two more patrol cars.

I walked up to the policeman who was questioning the old lady.

"I'll take over, Constable," I said. He nodded to me and stepped back, raising a gloved hand in acknowledgement. I took out my notebook and a pen.

"Ma'am, my name is Detective Sergeant Soames with CID. I apologise if the constable here has already asked you a lot of questions, but I do need to start from the beginning."

"That's alright, dear," she replied. "It's just that I have been worried for the poor girl for a while. She might come across a bit..." she paused. "Distasteful, but she is a nice creature most of the time."

"What is your name, ma'am?"

"Elsie, dear. Elsie Rhodes."

I wrote her name down. "Ms Rhodes, what do you mean by 'distasteful'?"

She waggled a finger at me. "Elsie, dear, please. It is the clothes she wears, mainly. She talks to me when I am working in the garden and she is out running. She comes up with those ear piece things in and wearing so little. It's not proper. Can I sit down, dear?"

There was a bench in her front garden, and I ushered her over there. She walked ahead of me, and was followed by the faint smell of mothballs and old clothes. I could almost hear her bones creak as she eased herself back onto the bench. Suppressing a grin at the irony, I wrote down 'runner, fitness' on my pad and sat down next to her.

"What made you call us, Ms Rhodes?"

"Be a dear, and call me Mrs if you must. Well I came out to put out the rubbish, you know? The men come by tomorrow to pick it up. Anyway, that Benjamin's dreadful car was on the drive with the engine running and the door open. That's not normal for them. Her car is usually there, and his is in the garage. Then I saw the front door was open, and I thought he had just run in to get something, but then I heard a scream from the house. I always thought he was a bad lot, but that settled it. Something was wrong, so I called 9-9-9. Is she okay?"

I chose my words carefully. I did not want to shock the old lady too much. "There has been an incident, Mrs Rhodes. You did right by calling us." I looked quickly at the note Cartwright had given me as I left. "Did you see Mr Wattler at all?"

"No. I just heard her. Christine, her name is. I didn't see anything other than what I have said. Besides, my eyes are not as good as they used to be. I thought it was better to call you lot than to go looking."

She was right there, and not just because of her vision. "Thank you, Mrs Rhodes. We might want to speak with you again." I waved to the man who had been talking to her. He approached. "Constable - ah…"

"Roberts, sir."

"Constable Roberts will take down your particulars, and we will be back in touch if our investigation requires it. Thank you for your assistance, Mrs Rhodes."

"That's alright, dear."

I left Roberts with Elsie Rhodes and headed back to the scene. Rickard had stopped vomiting and had clearly been checking adjacent residences. I called to him.

"No-one in, sir," he said. "Both neighbours' houses are empty at the moment, and the one behind them is for sale. I doubt anyone else heard anything."

I nodded thanks to Rickard and was about to re-enter number 72 when a black car with tinted windows pulled up in front of the house. A portable blue police light flashed on the dashboard. The door opened, and Detective Chief Superintendent Kwaku climbed from the vehicle.

I could not help but feel a twinge of uncertainty. DCS Kwaku was a figure not often seen, but well-known, and not so well-liked. His reputation preceded him as someone who trivialised cases to outsiders, while expecting more-than-human results from the men in the police force. It did not help that he tended to travel in dress uniform. I do not mean to sound racist when I say that the six foot three black man in full Met dress was a very imposing sight. Nonetheless, I approached as he straightened his uniform. I managed a "Sir-" before he cut me off with a raised hand.

"Let me see for myself," he said.

4

I stood at the door to the bedroom while DCS Kwaku looked at the scene. He was completely silent in his examination. The forensic team stood by me, nervously fiddling with their equipment. Carrey sat on the top step of the staircase, obviously ashamed of his earlier moment of weakness. I just felt awkward. Nothing about all this felt normal.

Three people at least had looked at the room so far, and yet we knew nothing for sure. Norton had discovered no sign of forced entry anywhere in the house, which had frankly been good enough for me, but then if Wattler had left the front door open, forced entry would hardly have been necessary.

Still, I wanted the forensic team in there. I wanted procedure followed, and I wanted to write this off as the horrific, self-destructive mess that it appeared to be. More than that, I wanted it confirmed as a horrific, self-destructive mess. I could intuit as well as the next person, but I liked using my intuition only as a basis for further investigation, and I would not be happy until everything had a factual backing to it.

Kwaku straightened, and I immediately became alert again. The forensic guys looked at me for a cue. Kwaku did not move, however, and simply stared at the writing on the wall. My shoulders slumped and I saw the fidgeting restart out of the corner of my eye.

I turned to look at Carrey. I felt that I should say something to him, but it was not the time. He would just have to spend a little more time screwing his toes into his shoes. I would speak to him later.

I looked back into the room and almost jumped, as DCS Kwaku had moved silently to stand right next to me. I suppressed the impulse and straightened up. He motioned for me to follow him and stepped past Carrey and down the steps. I waved to the forensic team to get back to work, and followed Kwaku out of the house. He did not say a word until he was standing next to the black car again, when he turned to look at me.

"Detective Sergeant Soames." It was a statement of fact, not a question. I wondered if he had known my name, or if he had asked someone. For some reason, the direct address made my skin crawl. "I want you to write a full report of this scene. Do not miss out a single fact, no matter how trivial or irrelevant it may appear to be. Deliver it to me - personally - no later than 1800 hours this evening."

"Yes, sir," I said, feeling my palms becoming clammy.

"Personally. Make sure of that. I will be expecting you."

Without a further word, he got back into his car and nodded to his driver. Instinctively, my wide eyes followed the line of his nod, and I saw both the driver and the vehicle's third occupant for just a second before the door slammed shut and the tinted windows obscured my view once again. The black car's engine started up and it pulled away, without any further acknowledgement of what had just happened or what was in the building behind me.

I stood by the side of the road for a moment. I could not actually process what had just happened. DCS Kwaku was my boss' boss' boss' boss. Despite that, he was not putting one of his own men onto the case, but was leaving me in charge, despite my relative inexperience, my rookie partner, and everything else that was odd about this situation.

What worried me even more was what he had seen. What was he looking for, that went beyond what the rest of us had picked up?

Even more strangely, why was Police Constable Norton in the car with him?

I turned back and headed for the house.

"Everything okay, Sarge?" asked Morley.

"Yeah, no problem. Do me a favour, Morley. Ask Roberts to wait here when he next comes by. I need to talk to him."

"Roberts, sir?"

"Yes, PC Roberts. He was interviewing the old lady."

"I don't know a PC Roberts, Sarge. Are you sure that was the name?"

"Of course I am. I thought you all knew one another." I turned to face the street where an ambulance had just pulled up. "Roberts," I called. No-one answered. "PC Roberts."

Several confused faces looked at me. One of the uniformed constables standing at the foot of the Wattler drive asked "Who, Sarge?" I did not have time for this. I stepped into the house and shouted for Carrey. As he descended the stairs I asked him about Roberts as well.

"I don't know him, sir. Is he new too?"

I sighed and sent Carrey out to look for the man while I headed back upstairs to see what forensics had. It seemed that my earlier premonition had been right - today was not going to be easy.

The forensic team were scouring the area around the two bodies. Blood samples were taken; the two dresses the woman had been holding were sealed into evidence bags, as was the stiletto shoe; notes were made about every detail to do with the crime.

"Murder-suicide?" I asked as I entered the room.

One of the team, who I recognised as a woman named Ackerman, looked up.

"Looks that way, sir," she said. "There's been no evidence found so far to contradict such a theory."

Something told me that, while the statement may have been true, it was also just too easy. I waved absently at Ackerman and she returned to her duties. I moved to where DCS Kwaku had stood, looking in the last direction I had seen him staring. I saw only what I had seen already - just from a different angle.

There was something that he had seen that we had all missed. There must be. If there was not, then nothing about this morning made sense any more. One of the forensic team, a man I did not know, got up to walk to the pile of equipment they had left away from the bodies. He crossed in front of the French doors that opened onto the balcony outside the bedroom and, as he did so, the sleeve of his plastic suit caught the thick gauze curtain that hung half-closed in front of the door.

My eyes, caught by the movement, flickered down to floor level. There.

"Hey," I called. Everyone turned to look at me, including the man who had hit the curtain. I pointed at the fabric near the floor. "Move that curtain out of the way again," I said.

He reached out and pulled it back, looking a little confused, but followed my gaze down to the floor. He looked up first at Ackerman and then at me. Ackerman stood, staring at the bottom of the curtain.

Underneath it was a partial footprint, sunken into the carpet and slightly muddy. This case had just become a lot more complicated.

5

The CID room at the station looked like any other. It was a riot of blandness, dull colours and musty smells. My desk stood against one wall, the light of the sun permanently in my eyes as I sat at it, and my back to many of my colleagues. We frequently spoke about moving the furniture around the room, but no-one ever seemed to get to it.

Somehow, finding myself back there and typing up a report after a day out in the field seemed very banal, particularly considering the unusual appearance of the DCS. One bit of detective work I never really appreciated was typing. Clearly someone else considered it a dull activity too, for some time after I had started, a stress ball struck me on the side of the head and bounced onto my desk.

"Was that really necessary?" I asked, turning to face Detective Inspector Harry Randall.

"No, but it was fun." He sat down and switched on his computer screen. I lobbed the stress ball back at him and he caught it.

"I'm short on time, man, sorry."

"Right, you caught the murder-suicide?"

"Yep. Got to write the report on it in the next hour. For The Quack."

"What?" The stress ball came flying at my head again. "Get out of here."

An inch from my head, I caught the ball. On a normal day I would brag that I was that good, despite the luck involved. Today, I just squeezed the ball and turned back to my desk.

"Seriously. I need to write, Harry."

"All right. I'll be at the Extended Living Room if you want to join me when you're done." He must have sensed that something was not right. It was not like him to give in so easily, but I could not complain this time.

"Thanks. Hold a pint for me."

"Done. Once I've finished my own paperwork."

"Cheers?" I clinked an imaginary glass over my shoulder towards his desk.

Harry snorted and we fell back into silence. I sat there trying to write, but stared at a page no more than one-third full. Not a word in half an hour. I could not concentrate. Everything had made such perfect sense until the footprint.

Reports from the police constables on the scene did not allow for a convenient explanation either. Very few people had apparently seen anything that I had not, and none had seemed to have any further suggestions beyond my own. Those neighbours that had been around that day, Mrs Rhodes excepted, were particularly ignorant of the events, but from what I had been told that was not unusual in Stapely Drive. The houses on either side of the Wattler's were still empty, and things might improve when the residents of those properties got home, but somehow I doubted it.

So who was the mystery interloper, and what reason did he have for being on the scene of a murder? I could no longer consider it a murder-suicide until it was proven as such - or proven to be something else. I could not get rid of a nagging feeling that, somehow, the whole situation was more than it seemed.

There was one other problem that might or might not be related. Since I had left him with Elsie Rhodes, no-one had seen Constable Roberts. Two mysteries arose from that. Firstly, who on earth was the man who had identified himself as Roberts? Secondly, could he be responsible for the footprint in the bedroom?

Lastly on my list of enigmas - at least that I could tackle for now - was the fact that Norton had not found any evidence of forced entry. Did that mean that at least one of the Wattlers knew the owner of the footprint?

I was getting genuinely nervous about submitting my report to DCS Kwaku. The more I wrote, the more holes the case seemed to develop. Most people do not realise how tiring investigations can be. I could feel my mental acuity failing, and my mind was trying to answer questions instead of writing the facts that I already knew.

In the end, if I am completely honest, fear overrode my distraction, and I managed to focus for the half-hour I needed in order to write something that detailed the event. I spent ten minutes reading over it three times and with each reading I became more convinced that Kwaku was going to be unimpressed, and he was not a man you wanted to annoy.

I sighed and looked at the clock. The minute hand ticked up to the ten. 1750 hours. I got up and headed for the Quack's office. I heard voices from inside, so I knocked on the door and sat down next to it to wait. I was there for no more than two minutes when I heard Kwaku's voice call out "Come." I knocked again and opened the door.

Detective Chief Superintendent Kwaku sat in his chair with a large file on his desk. He was as impeccably dressed as he had been earlier, although his hat topped the coat-stand that stood beside the door. However, it was not his imposing figure that stopped me dead in the doorway. It was not even the bottle of whiskey that adorned the desk, and the half-finished glass in his hand, which was not what I had expected from a man like him.

Behind and to the left of DCS Kwaku's chair stood Police Constable Roberts.

6

"Forgive me, sir, but I am a little bit-"

"Confused?" DCS Kwaku cut me off. I almost fell over when he smiled and looked at me expectantly. What was going on?

"Misinformed." That was not strictly true, but I did not want Kwaku to think me completely stupefied, although I realised that it might already be too late for that.

"Oh? About what?"

Damn. "About your colleague here. The men at the station indicated that there was no such officer by the name of PC Roberts that they knew of, and he disappeared completely after interviewing a witness at the scene."

"Yes, I'm afraid he did. Please, Detective Soames, take a seat."

Kwaku had made me feel distinctly uncomfortable by now, and he was one very cool customer. Nothing in his eyes betrayed anything other than a mild amusement at my situation. I felt myself flush and quickly sat in the chair facing him, hoping to cover my embarrassment.

"I must apologise, Sergeant. I have you at a significant disadvantage, and I must not make fun of you."

With a voice as deep and commanding as Kwaku's, I could not imagine him making fun of anyone or any thing. I looked at him, trying not to make it obvious that I was attempting to read his expression. I could not detect anything other than sincerity. I wondered if The Quack was not quite so much of a glory-hugging bastard as many thought, unless he was exceptionally good at hiding it at second meetings.

"I am afraid that is true," I said. I almost forgot myself, but then added: "Sir."

"Then we must do something to dispel that disadvantage. At least, a little of it." This time he did not disguise the humour in his voice and yet I felt that it was not directed at me, but at the situation itself.

"Thank you, sir. I would appreciate that."

"Roberts, if you would." Kwaku did not turn as he spoke. He stared at me so intensely, that I was about to open my mouth to remind him that my name was Oliver when PC Roberts reached up behind him and slid the blinds down, flicking them shut and blocking out the creeping dusk outside. He then dimmed the lights in the office, closed the air ventilator and locked the door. If I had not been so baffled by all of this, I might have been afraid.

"Detective Sergeant Oliver Soames. Born in London, England. Son of Thomas Dean Soames and Anne Louise Wright. Father murdered when you were twelve years old. You lived with your mother until you were twenty-two and then you moved out and joined the Metropolitan Police Service. You said this was because your friend Harry Randall encouraged you to join with him, but I suspect an ulterior motive. Were you afraid that seeking some form of posthumous justice for your father by helping to catch criminals yourself might not be an acceptable reason to join the force?"

He had no dossier that I could see, and his eyes still never left mine, even when my own flicked to PC Roberts. Roberts' were starting straight ahead, alert and focussed. Before I could speak, the DCS carried on.

"Harry has surpassed you in the force, and not particularly because he is any more capable - actually, he is not - but because you hold yourself back, probably because you are in a position that feels safe to you. You live alone and have no long-term partner, though you do socialise with other people of both genders. You prefer a life of solitude, but you are not socially awkward. Most of the time. You respect and, I think, idolise Chief Superintendent Whittaker, because it was he who caught your father's killer and secured his conviction at the subsequent trial. I believe you were slightly disappointed when you were assigned to CID because it meant you were to be reporting up *my* chain of command and not his."

He was right on every factual count - and his conjecture was only a stone's throw from the truth, at worst. I just sat there, without saying a word. My mouth may have been open. I honestly cannot remember.

"You communicate with your mother by typed letter only, and beside Harry and occasionally his sister, you do not have any friends whom you would consider close. How am I doing, Detective Sergeant?"

"You are apparently extremely well-informed, sir," I said. I think my voice sounded a little strangled. I tripped over the word 'extremely' the first time around, and had to turn back for a second go.

"Thank you. I say all this so that you will understand the depth of the research that my chain of command puts into our recruits. You see, I am rather a unique individual in the Metropolitan Police Service. You know my face. You have seen me on television. You think that I am enacting some kind of modern-day gold rush, stealing the public glory for cases from the individuals who do the work. All of this is true, because it is an image that I cultivate most carefully, although not without great sorrow at the way I must appear to all of you. Earlier today, you discovered the reason why, even though you do not know it yet."

He nodded meaningfully at the report that I still held in my hands. It took me a moment to get his meaning, but then I muttered an apology and handed it to him. He opened it, skimmed a few lines and then handed it to Roberts. Kwaku sat there looking at me as Roberts read the report more thoroughly. Kwaku's desk clock ticked away the time and, as I grew increasingly nervous, the ticking seemed to get louder, until it felt like the sands of time were being counted inside my own mind, grain by grain slipping away.

With no further word, Roberts flipped the report into his other hand and fed it into an industrial shredder far more advanced than the one we had in the CID office. I started in surprise.

"You found unexplained anomalies in the case. You do know your work, Soames, and you do it exceedingly well. I asked you to report everything and you did. Everything that you could prove. You then created bullet-points that require further investigation, which is exactly what I was looking for. I will now answer two of them for you."

"No, Police Constable Roberts is not responsible for the footprint that you saw. Yes, Police Constable Roberts is an official member of the British Security Services, but not quite as you saw him today. He works for a department that exists solely to plug the holes that you spotted. Welcome to the Metropolitan Special Circumstance Executive."

7

"I beg your pardon?" I was not quite sure that I had heard right. "The what?"

"The Metropolitan Special Circumstance Executive, or MSCE, exists to step in where there are forces at work that the regular police force, CID or even Special Branch are not equipped to deal with. There are a great variety of misnomers that cover our work. Some say paranormal, others magic, and some even argue in religious terms. Our work is none of the above. We simply deal with people who are different to the norm."

"Pardon me, sir, but have I gone mad?"

"No, Soames, you have not. I will demonstrate."

I watched Kwaku switch on a video camera that faced me. He turned and nodded to PC Roberts, who moved, for the first time since he had shredded my report, and came around to my side of the desk. I jumped to my feet and prepared to defend myself.

"Do not worry, Sergeant." There was a slight tone of command in Kwaku's voice that oddly set me at ease. "We are not going to harm you, and I promise you with all sincerity that you are not losing your mind. Roberts here, or Creeker as we call him, is one of the people we were just discussing. You are completely safe, but everyone needs proof of what we are dealing with when they first come into contact with us."

"I want you to do three things. Look at the clock, so that you are fully aware of the time at this exact moment. Then say something unique: tell us something about yourself or your life that you have absolutely never told anyone ever before. Finally, just trust us and allow your mind to be open to what follows."

I did what he told me. It did not seem like I had much of a choice, and the police station was monitored by CCTV cameras, so there was not much that he could do without someone finding out.

The clock on the wall showed twelve minutes past six. I thought for a moment about something he could not possibly know. It was not an easy task, given the fact that he had essentially reduced my life to a series of statements not five minutes previously.

"When I was fourteen, I had a crush on my chemistry teacher." I tried very hard not to flush again. It was a ridiculous thing to say, but it was the only thing I could think of that they should have no way of knowing. If Harry or CS Whittaker or someone like that was involved, and this was some kind of bizarre practical joke, their knowledge could be almost limitless through association.

"Okay," said Kwaku. He did not bat an eyelid or comment on my revelation. "Now relax. We will prove all of this in just a few moments."

I understood afterwards why the video was running. Once Kwaku had finished talking I began to tell my life story, in much the same way he had earlier. The thing is, it was not my life. I did not remember a word of what I had said even two seconds after I said it, but I was absolutely convinced that it was an autobiographical account. The only thing I was conscious of was Roberts or Creeker or whatever he was called holding my arm for the duration.

When he released his grip, I immediately forgot the last thing I had said, or anything that had happened since Kwaku had said 'in just a few moments'. I could have sworn blind that no time had passed at all.

However, when I looked at the clock, it showed nineteen minutes past six. I gaped, unable to comprehend how seven minutes had just vanished. Then Creeker turned the video on and played it back. There I was, exactly where I stood now. I saw myself look at the clock, think, and then declare the crush I had had on my chemistry teacher. There was absolutely no doubt that it was real.

Then Creeker took my arm, and I explained how I was a forty-two year-old woman who had grown up in County Cork and moved to London with my twenty-five-year-old boyfriend to pursue a career as a bespoke milliner. He had left me when I became pregnant, and I had been forced to give the child up for adoption due to the financial crisis. It went on for almost exactly seven minutes. Then Creeker took his arm away and the video stopped on my astonished expression as I looked up at the clock.

Kwaku looked kindly at me. "Creeker can implant any personality he wishes on another person. It is an unsettling experience, as you just found out, but the subject never remembers what happened. In the meantime, they will believe, with absolute conviction, anything that he imprints on their mind. However, he must maintain physical contact to achieve this. You can put your gloves back on now."

This last sentence was to Creeker. He pulled a pair of black leather gloves over his hands and stepped back. There was a faint hint of a smile on his face.

I realised that I had noticed the gloves at the crime scene. I assumed they were for warmth, but he was the only officer wearing them, and they were far too fine a quality to be department issue.

"So, Detective Sergeant, the question is whether you accept that some things can happen that, with your current knowledge and social upbringing, you may not give credence to. Secondly, are you open-minded enough to explore, learn and accept these things? Thirdly, will you help us against those with more malevolent purposes than Police Constable Roberts here? It is, of course, entirely up to you."

"What happens if I refuse?" I asked.

"We will allow you to forget all of this. It is not out of our power. If you can accept that, you have already answered two of the questions."

I nodded.

"Very well then. What about the third?"

8

Half an hour later, I found myself in what was known affectionately to the CID as the Extended Living Room, and to everyone else as The Last Glass pub. I was sat with Harry listening to him ramble about the case he was working on, but none of it was really going in.

My mind was focussed on everything I had just learned. My hands were more engaged in a kind of production line motion that involved picking up the pint of ale in front of me, draining some of the glass, putting it back on the table and then picking it up again. I did not even take in the taste of the drink.

I imagined that the revelation probably gave me a similar feeling to that of discovering a new law of physics, and trying to work out how to prove it to yourself. My whole world had been turned upside down in about fifteen minutes, and I did not know how to react. Yet there seemed to be little doubt of the veracity of Kwaku's words. Creeker's little demonstration seemed beyond doubt.

Questions exploded into my head. How many of these people were there? What could they do? How dangerous could they be? How would you find one if he did not want to be discovered? The simple fact that these people existed, and that there was some kind of black ops police force dedicated to combatting them would normally have me impressed and excited. Thing is, I was in the middle of it all, and that made it different.

"Hey, Oli." Harry whacked my arm and I snapped to alertness.

"Sorry. My mind wandered for a moment."

Harry tapped his glass. He had drunk about a third of his pint. My glass was empty.

"The Quack really got to you, huh?" he asked. "Sure, it's a school night and I'm going slow, but you never drink faster than me."

"It's just been a really long day. That murder was none too pretty, you know."

I waved to Bouncing Betty, the bartender and daughter of the owner. She finished up the order she was working on and pulled me another pint. She walked down the bar, her tight, low-cut top working hard to validate her nickname, came out to our table, and put the glass in front of me. I handed over a few coins. It was an unspoken agreement between us that she kept the change from what I gave her.

"Rough day, babe?" she asked.

I nodded. "Something like that."

"Grab us a pack of dry roast, Betty," said Harry.

The peanuts appeared immediately, and she took two more coins from Harry. She hovered for a second, waiting for our usual banter, and when nothing was forthcoming she raised an eyebrow and walked away.

"Go slow on that one, Oli, and eat these." Harry tore the pack of nuts open, took a handful, and pushed the rest towards me. My production line of drinking resumed, but with an occasional deviation to eat nuts.

"The Quack chew you out?" Harry asked.

"Let's just say he trashed my report."

"Damn, that's cold. I saw you writing that thing. Looked like a thesis."

"There were too many holes. Most significantly, the presence of a footprint that did not belong to one of the victims combined with no forced entry."

"Oh ho," said Harry. "A double murder then?"

"Quite possibly."

"You got a photograph of the print? I know a guy who is a genius with boots. He's a hill climber and could identify a pair by a good print. Maybe shoes too?"

"Definitely a boot, I'd say, judging by weight and sole style. Would you show it to him? It's in the forensic file I've put together. There was a copy in the report, but DCS Kwaku... kept that."

"Sure. I'll send it to him tomorrow."

"Thanks, Harry. You may well turn out to be a lifesaver."

What I wanted to say was 'Don't bother. The print may well turn out to be from a ghost'. However, Kwaku had sworn me to secrecy about the MSCE, and I did not know my feelings about it well enough to break that commitment just yet. Also, it just did not feel like something I wanted to make fun of.

"You going to be okay, Oli?"

"Yeah. Yeah, I'll be fine. You know what, I think I'm going to head home and get a little shut-eye. It has just been a really long, ugly day. I knew I shouldn't have crawled out of bed this morning."

"I hear that." He looked at my mostly untouched pint. "You okay to drive?"

"Sure. Only the one. I'm fine."

"You want that?" He nodded at the glass.

"In a doggy bag? No, Harry, you have it."

"Thanks."

"See you tomorrow."

"Yeah, yeah."

I had turned to leave when Harry's voice called me back.

"Oli. It's a pussy thing to say, but text me when you get home? You look like hell."

I nodded and left. I actually managed a slight grin when I heard Betty slap Harry's arm for his language. She ran a tight shop when it came to respectability, despite her flirting. I had often thought about hanging around for the end of her shift. She used her assets well, and it was difficult not to think of that most times, but I had too much respect for her.

Fortunately I knew a number, and there was nothing respectable about it at all.

9

I called on the way home, and the girl arrived an hour later. I opened the door and she walked in, standing so that I could not close the door. She glanced around, and then gave me a meaningful look. I held out a small roll of notes. She counted the money and nodded. She stepped in, closed the door behind her, and took out her phone. I knew that the text was a confirmation that she had been paid and could see no immediate danger in the flat.

I could not shake a moment of sadness that such precautions were necessary. Equally, as sometimes happened, I felt disappointed in myself that I was doing this. I was not a bad-looking man, and should have been able to find a partner, but my heart was committed to someone, and we were not going to become an item any time soon.

I put the thoughts out of my head and looked at the girl to see who the agency had sent me. They knew me, and I had a long-standing arrangement that they never sent me the same girl twice. This one was a blonde. Her hair was hidden under a beanie hat, and she covered her body with a red coat with a wide belt. It only fell to her knees, and I looked at the start of a pair of shapely, stockinged legs, which ended in a pair of black stiletto heels.

The heels reminded me for a second of the fate of Benjamin Wattler, and for a moment I lost my composure as I imagined what it must take to kill yourself with a high-heeled shoe, however sharp the heel.

When the girl had finished texting, she looked up at me and smiled. The smile was warm, but I had used working girls enough to recognise the sign of effort in their expressions. I knew that my agency was not the best or kindest, but I could not afford a really good one. She had probably had an appointment not long before. I tried not to think about it.

"I'm Maria," she said. The accent was seductively Eastern European. I had a weakness for that sound. Her voice was sweet, and younger than she looked, but that was okay.

"Tim," I said. "Tim Harvey."

I used a pseudonym for the service, though I was not sure whether it was out of embarrassment or some absurd idea of trying to keep the activity from someone. Not that anyone was likely to find out anyway, and if they did, I wasn't sure I cared.

"And what can I do for you, Tim Harvey?" asked Maria.

She was good, I'll give her that. Her voice held an enticing combination of sensuality and naughtiness, with just a hint of pleading.

On some occasions, these encounters were almost romantic in their gentleness. They became evenings of giggles, cries of pleasure, and soft moans. I would be the first person to admit that, with time to think about what I was doing, I was probably a little awkward in the bedroom, and this could lead to friendly banter, and deeper moments.

Though it seems callous, even to me, I was always thinking of someone else on those nights.

Tonight, however, was not going to be like that. I needed release. Maria stepped forwards and let her coat fall open. The fur lining parted and revealed a black bustier, thong, and suspender belt. The straps of the belt held up the stockings which were topped with lace bands around slender but toned thighs.

I felt myself harden as my eyes undressed her. Her pale skin and blue eyes seemed to accent the outlines of the dark lingerie she wore. Unbidden, my eyes fell to her breasts, pushed up by the form of the bustier. The soft flesh was inviting, and she pushed her chest out a little as she watched my gaze.

She pulled her hat off, and her blonde hair cascaded down. She arranged it quickly, and it framed her face, making her even more alluring. She pouted gently with maroon-coloured lips, and I gave in.

Clothes came off in a controlled frenzy. Mine were tossed every which way in the room, and hers ended up in a pile - almost neat - at the end of the bed. I did not recognise her perfume, but it intoxicated me.

I did not bother to take in her naked form, but pulled her to me. Her breasts were medium-sized, and squashed pleasingly into my chest. Our mouths and tongues met and parted again and again. I gripped her buttocks hard in my hands and felt the roughness of her pubic hair pressing against my thigh.

She pulled away and sat back on my bed. Her breasts fell gently to either side in a satisfying indication that they were not fake. She put her feet up and spread her legs wide. I stared at the carefully trimmed hair that pointed down to the wet lips below it. She leaned towards me and flicked her tongue suggestively. I shook my head. I played around, but I played safe. She could not hide the slight fall in her expression. She must be new, I decided.

Instead of going down on her, I opened a drawer by my bed and pulled out a flavoured condom. Strawberry, the packet claimed. Despite curiosity, I had never tasted one myself, but the girls seemed to prefer them. I tossed the wrapper aside, pulled the condom on, and stood by the bed as Maria repositioned herself and wrapped her mouth around me.

I enjoyed the sensation - I always do - but I was distracted. I needed to be doing something, rather that just standing and receiving, however good it felt. I let her continue for a few moments, but pulled away.

I pushed her back onto the bed and leaned down over her. Holding myself up on one hand, I use my other to try to press myself inside her. I missed a couple of times, and she had to reach down and guide me in. I gasped as I felt her surround me, and began to thrust back and forth, but yet again I found myself somewhere else.

I flipped us over, and lay back while she rode me and I stared at the ceiling. My only motions were my body's instinctual bucking to meet her as she bounced up and down on me. She tried to get my attention - I know that. She went slower then faster, then harder, even to the point where her motion became a little painful. She scratched my chest and slapped what of my arse she could reach.

When I went soft, she got off me and worked with her mouth again. She managed to arouse me again and sat back on me, facing the other way this time.

As I looked at her from behind, it was as though I saw the snaking straps of a white bra circle her back and fasten. Instead of seeing my erection sliding inside her, I saw a white thong cover her. Then both items of clothing suddenly became soaked in red.

I cried out and covered my face. Facing away from me, she must have thought that I was reaching orgasm, for I heard her begin to shout out encouragement. Instead, frightened out of my mind, I sat up and roughly pulled her up and off me. She turned, looked at my face, and then slapped it, hard. I watched her pull away from me, fearful, and begin to cry with now-wide eyes.

10

I apologised to the girl and she left. She rang the doorbell two minutes later and there was an awkward moment as I handed her phone back to her through the door without taking the chain off. Her face was streaked with tears, and her make-up had run badly. I heard the four-inch heels hurry back down the corridor and into the stairwell.

I stood in a scalding shower for at least quarter of an hour. When I went in, my skin was red with shame. I had never before treated a girl so badly, and I felt terrible about it. By the time I began to wash, the bathroom was filled with steam, and my fingers were wrinkled by the water.

I cleaned up without really thinking about it, pulled on a pair of boxers and sat on the edge of the bed. My vision was blurred and my mind would not focus.

I logged on to my laptop and got up while the machine hummed and blinked awake. I went to my kitchen and put on the coffee-maker, thumbing the button to make the coffee strong. I washed my face again while it brewed and stared at my reflection in the mirror. I told myself again and again that I was not mad. I'm not sure that I believed it, but it made me feel better for a moment. I watched the droplets of water trail down my face like so many fingertips stroking me. I found much more escape in the sight and the cool feel of the drops rolling across my skin than I had done in the arms of the escort.

I glanced at the newspaper which I had left on the bathroom shelf that morning, which was normally the only time of day I had to read it. Nothing ground-breaking. Politics annoyed me, as so much of it was 'politics', not diplomacy or representation. I had read the war correspondent's article that morning. My local councillor made the news over a new recycling scheme. A company called Endrell Associates had gone into administration after losing a malpractice lawsuit, threatening to cost its shareholders a lot of money. The sports news did not interest me.

The beeping of the coffee-maker split my reverie and I snatched a towel from the rack. Mug on the sideboard; one spoonful of sugar; one small top-up just to be sure; grab coffee pot and pour in coffee to half way; stir coffee to mix in sugar; fill mug; coffee pot back into maker; switch maker off; take a sip of coffee. The familiarity of the process was pleasing, and I could somehow sink into it more easily than anything else I had done so far that night.

Time to go to work.

Closing the door to my bedroom, I put the laptop onto the small table in my living area, sat down, and opened up three internet tabs. In the first, I set Google to searching for the Metropolitan Special Circumstance Executive. In the second, I set a second instance of Google to searching for Detective Chief Superintendent Kwaku but specified special ops as a search term. In the third, I loaded up my local cinema's showing times on the off-chance that I could catch a midnight showing and wind myself down again once I was done with this.

I closed the first tab within thirty seconds. The MSCE search brought up nothing other than board papers for banks or committees. As an acronym, it only came up with various Masters of Science courses or other forms of training. It was a complete dead-end.

The third tab showed that there was nothing on at my local cinema that night. It was closed for routine maintenance. I swapped to iTunes and started *The Karate Kid* downloading. The

2010 remake, not the 1984 version, but it was the first thing I saw that I could lose myself in.

The second tab was the one that needed the most work. Filtering through the results was challenging as Kwaku had so many public appearances related to cases. I skipped the videos as I knew they would get me riled up. Kwaku's habit of being the public face of every challenging case pissed me off as much as the next cop.

Still, he appeared to have revealed a new side of himself. I did not know how much I credited his statement that he only acted the way he did as a cover for his alternate persona, but then I was not about to contradict it either. Obviously there was a lot more going on here than I was aware of, and I would take everything with a pinch of salt until I knew more.

Instead, I focussed on looking for anything that would indicate his involvement in something other than 'regular business'. My search did not prove to be very fruitful. Variations of special ops all brought up useless pages - everything from paintball sites to army-related pages, and even charities. Special Branch bore little more fruit. In a last ditch attempt, I actually tried looking for his name against black ops. I don't know what I expected to find. Black ops are called that for a reason. However, I did come across one page that gave me a little more insight than I expected.

It appeared that a Corporal Kwaku had been dishonourably discharged from the British Army and the article that I read on it implied involvement in a black op of some description, though details were not forthcoming. I was amazed that even this much had made it onto the internet, but then I supposed that anything could be found if you looked hard enough.

There was a picture on the site of a man in army fatigues being escorted. He had a hand up to obscure his face from the camera, but the nose shape and skin tone were very similar, if not exact. It was not enough to form conclusive proof that Kwaku was an ex black operative, but it was enough for me to suspect it.

I do not know how long I had sat there, staring at the picture and willing it to tell me more, when the door to my flat was kicked down and three men clad in black entered. I jumped to my feet and tried to find something to defend myself with. I had finished my mug of coffee, and the pot, while still hot, was too far away. I considered a chair, but that was just impractical.

The man in front looked quickly around the flat and pointed at my laptop.

"Take it," he said, and one of the men moved forwards.

"Now wait just a minute-" I took a step towards him, but found myself face-to-face with the business end of a Walther .40. The man who had moved took my laptop and disappeared from the flat. The third man moved back and closed the door while the one who appeared to be in charge kept his gun on me.

"DS Soames," said the man. I nodded, and he held up a mobile phone - an older clamshell model. "Catch."

He flipped the phone to me and I caught it. Within just a couple of my now very fast heartbeats, it rang. The man nodded once. I flipped the phone open and raised it cautiously to my ear.

"Hello?"

"Detective Sergeant Soames." I recognised Kwaku's voice. "You are a difficult man. You did not react the way we predicted. We expected the girl to be with you for longer, but now we need to bring you in and induct you. Immediately. Mr Harding and his associates will bring you to me. Do not be alarmed, Soames. I apologise for the necessary force, and for the nature of these proceedings. We did not expect you to go searching quite so quickly and had to shut you down. Our reasons will become clear. I will see you shortly."

The line clicked and I closed the phone again. I tossed it back to the man I presumed to be Mr Harding.

"I guess I'm coming with you then."

11

We drove in absolute silence. I had been in cars with awkward atmospheres before, of course, but there was something different about this one. Within five minutes, I wanted to be absolutely anywhere except where I was. The only movement throughout the journey was made by the man who had taken my laptop. He sat there typing faster than I ever thought possible.

The car was like Kwaku's - a black, tinted Audi - but it was clearly incredibly customised. The ride was almost completely silent, with only the slightest indication that we were moving much of the time. The constant clicking from my laptop's keyboard actually started to irritate me, but some sense of self-pride stopped me from asking questions, or letting on that I was in any way uncomfortable.

I tried to pay attention to where we were going, but it was dark by this point and the tint in the windows dulled the view still further, and I lost track. Eventually we pulled into an underground parking garage, well-secured and guarded. The driver flashed a permit out the window as we arrived, a mirror was passed under the car, and the boot was checked.

We pulled into a parking space and piled out of the car. My laptop was returned to me, and we continued our silent convoy into the elevator. Mr Harding inserted a key into the lift's operating panel and selected the Penthouse floor. I started to fidget a little as the doors closed and I felt myself becoming more and more anxious. Whatever was up there had better be good.

The elevator started moving down.

I started and looked around at the men surrounding me, but they appeared to be completely unaffected by what was happening, and maintained their passive expressions. We dropped what felt like a good eight floors before the lift slowed and stopped. There was an unexpectedly standard elevator 'bing' and the doors slid open.

With all the secrecy and security, I was expecting to walk into some kind of futuristic command centre, like the Agency in *Men In Black*. What I actually saw could not have been further from that. The room we faced was not dissimilar to the police station offices, although it was more open plan. Bright strip lights hung from the ceiling, enclosed in light blue casings that leant the room a cold, clinical feel. The walls were painted an eggshell blue and the floor was bare stone.

I was ushered out of the lift by Mr Harding, and I followed him through an organised spider's web of desks. I estimated that there was space for about forty people, although there were only five there that I could see. Two looked up from their work, apparently noticed me, recognised that I was Harding's charge and then went back to work. One looked like he was asleep, and the other two ignored me, deep in conversation with each other.

As we approached a large steel door, Mr Harding turned to me and said: "This is where I leave you, Sergeant." He entered a keycode into a pad on the wall and the door opened automatically. He gestured for me to proceed through the door, but there was no kindness or politeness in his eyes. The action was a mere formality.

I passed through, and the door closed behind me with a quiet clunk as it locked back into place. I found myself in a room that looked like some kind of archive room. Filing cabinets covered the far wall, and there was a large, raised table, which was covered with papers and books, and seemed to be built into the floor.

At the far end of the room, behind the table, DCS Kwaku stood up from a desk, replaced the cap on his pen, and closed the book in front of him.

"Sergeant Soames." His voice reverberated oddly around the room, sounding almost distorted. I realised that all the sounds I was hearing were echoing back from unexpected corners. Whether or not it was a trick to disarm people, the effect was definitely unnerving.

"I apologise for the manner of your arrival," Kwaku continued. "We do not normally enact such dramatic measures, but it was necessary to stop your online search activities as quickly as possible. I appreciate that you wanted to find out about us but, as you undoubtedly discovered, there is no information about this organisation available on the internet, and we wish to keep it that way. From our experience, failed searches lead to questions on forums, and those questions then become an exposure risk."

"That's understood, sir. To be honest, I think I wanted confirmation that I hadn't completely lost it. I believe I got that more firmly through a complete dearth of information than I would have done if I had found even a holding page. I would not have asked anything publicly."

"Perhaps not knowingly, no. The question is what is public nowadays. We conduct the majority of our information exchange over encrypted servers, but you will also find that a lot of our data is stored on paper. It is one of the best defences in the information age."

"That makes sense."

"Do you write?"

The question caught me off guard. "I'm sorry?"

"With a pen. Have you actually handwritten anything besides a scrawled police memo recently, or do you only type, as you do to your mother?"

"I type, sir. I am out of the way of writing."

Kwaku opened a drawer in the side of the raised table. A selection of pens of all varieties were laid out as if in a display case. I stared at them for a moment. Some were simple black cylinders with pen nibs, and obviously took ink cartridges. Others were quick-dry gel pens, or fancy biros. One or two were ornate-looking fountain pens with levers for sucking up ink. All had their lids next to them, and the last type lay next to ink bottles.

The DCS looked up at me, gestured to the pens, and made to leave the room. He called back over his shoulder as he walked away.

"Get back into it."

12

Very little needed to be said for me to accept the necessity of the extreme security. The methodology was a little more peculiar, but it made a lot of sense. The information age gave us an awful lot of advantages and opportunities that were not available before. On the flipside, hacking scares, the questionable security of social networking sites, and an emphasis on freedom of information had made hiding anything on the internet almost impossible.

The filing cabinets, I learned, essentially contained case files. However, these were very different to an average police case file. The MSCE files went into detail about subjects' abilities and psychological profiles. They were not just rap sheets, but also scientific analyses, personality dissections, and threat assessments.

Some of the subjects had long and detailed forms, whereas others had only shown up once. Files were organised first into ability type - identified by the two digits that began their individual six-digit code numbers - and then into risk level, from low to extreme. No-one with abilities was considered to be a no-risk subject. I also learned quickly that all ability-possessing people were on file, including those working for the MSCE, both in the office here - nicknamed the Penthouse - and in the field.

However, these last subjects had sealed files that could only be viewed by high-ranking officers of the MSCE, and then only with valid cause. I was shown the identities of those officers with abilities, and then the files were returned to a specific, biometrically-locked safe. The label on the front said 'Natives'.

To be honest, the names all but left my head as quickly as they had entered. Norton and Creeker were the only two whose names I recognised, and I recalled references to a man named Whistler, and a file with a big 'Closed' stamp on the front for an individual named Daedalus.

The most disarming thing was the age of some of the files. I had assumed, given its nature and presentation, that the MSCE was a young organisation. However, I pulled out files dating back decades. I saw one particularly ancient-looking file for an individual, known as The Old Man, which I discovered dated back to 1537. It was huge and contained many files for various aliases. The first few were recorded either on unbound parchment in carefully-formed, handwritten script, or printed by what must have been amongst the earliest of printing presses.

There was a modern file attached to it which summarised the information. It turned out that, for all the papers in the original folder, pretty much nothing was known about The Old Man, other than the fact that he simply did not age. He was, to go by the earliest accounts, almost eight hundred years old, but there was no image to confirm how old he really was.

I had also been left with an 'Internal Operations Briefing Packet', which was apparently standard for new recruits. I learned that all MSCE members were current or ex-'home security officers'. In other words, I presumed, everyone here was or had been a policeman of some sort.

"It is quite the wake-up call, is it not."

Mr Harding walked up to me and smiled. To my surprise, with his commanding tone lost his voice was actually quite soft and gentle.

"Yes. Yes, it is," I replied.

Our voices still echoed oddly around the room. I realised as he approached, that his voice sounded no louder or different to me. It occurred to me then that the room might be designed in such a way that anyone speaking could be heard equally well wherever a listener stood. If that were the case, I was unsure whether it was good security, paranoia, or just a freak of the original design.

"I remember when I first saw all this," said Harding. "I did not adapt as easily as you have, but then Creeker was on assignment and not at hand to show me the truth. It is easier once you have experienced an ability first hand. Plus, Creeker can actually leave a little piece of personality. Recruits are not told that until they have accepted the position. Inside you there is a little bit of imprinted 'persuasion'. It makes it easier for you to believe all of this. It would be too much for many people to accept at first, and it is… messy when we have to make someone forget."

I decided it was best not to ask about that, but instead came to the one question that I had inexplicably omitted to ask until this point.

"What does this have to do with me? Why now?"

Mr Harding smiled again, but this time it was all back to business. "Allow me to present Ashley. She will be overseeing your work until such a time as it is decided that you are able to function in a fully autonomous capacity."

He seemed to almost melt away. There was something slimy in his demeanour and apparent ingratiation. Despite that, I could not help feeling that he was an ally - one to be feared, should I betray the trust that had been granted me, but one who could be relied on if that did not happen.

At any other time, I would have been struck dumb by the woman who he gave way to. She was staggeringly beautiful, although clearly a few years older than me. Long, dark hair stretched down her back and piercing blue eyes appeared to assess me as she walked up. Her black shirt was unbuttoned just far enough to indicate that she had a substantial bust, and her hips swayed provocatively as she moved.

Ashley was a name I had seen on the MSCE 'Native' files - an employee with an ability, though of course I was unaware of its nature. As a result, rather than becoming aroused by her beauty, I rather became wary of what I might leave vulnerable in myself.

In doing so, I realised why Natives were not described. A certain natural distrust would be helpful in an organisation that had to remain secret.

"Sergeant Soames. It is a pleasure to meet you," said Ashley. Her voice had a similar Eastern European accent to that of the escort girl, but had a more sultry quality. "Allow me to introduce myself. My name is Ashley, and I am what you might call a founding partner of the organisation. In its modern form, I mean." I got the sense that she considered this last statement to be something of an in-joke, but I could not see it.

"Between myself, Kwaku and one other that you may meet one day, we evaluate the early work of a new recruit and decide how best to use him henceforth. From what Kwaku tells me, it sounds as though you will be a most able field agent, but then we have been wrong before, and you may find yourself working analysis, and watching for news reports that suggest a Stranger is discovering or displaying his or her ability."

"But I am getting ahead of myself. You are wondering why you were brought here. Let me explain." Ashley beckoned me to follow, and we walked to what appeared to be a small meeting room with a round table, four chairs, and bottles of water set on a cupboard to one side, all fronted by a large glass window. As we approached, I caught myself staring at the fluid motion of her legs and hips, and hoped the agents working at the desks had not decided to look up and take note at that moment.

The room seemed cut into the wall in the side of the room, but as I stepped past the doorway, a glass panel slid closed behind us, and what little noise had come in from the main room vanished.

"It is quite simple, to be honest," she continued. "Recruits are brought in when they show sufficient aptitude to work for this department and when they approach a case involving someone with an ability. You are involved in such a case now - the murders you saw this morning."

"They are both murders then?"

"Yes."

"Who committed them? How do you know that it is someone... special?"

"The answer to the first is for you to discover. We do not yet know. It is not someone we have encountered before." She handed me an empty file, much like the ones from the cabinets. However, instead of a name, the tab simply indicated an eight digit case number. I also noticed a blank space for a six digit subject number, presumably for the archives.

"This is your first case - you need to do your job. That is why you are here. The answer to the second question is that one of our agents can sense most abilities when they are used. He saw the scene this morning and identified a new scent."

"Roberts?"

"No. No-one possesses more than one ability. Let us just say that your nickname of 'Sniffer' for PC Norton is not so unfounded."

All of a sudden, several mysteries in my head cleared up, including one or two I only thought of as I realised the answers to them. It certainly explained why Norton was as effective as he was at analysing crime scenes, but also why he was only at some, and why he had been in Kwaku's car at the Wattlers' house.

"Why do you tell me that?"

"Simply because you will meet Norton a lot during the course of your work with us, and you need to react normally. He is the one Native that we identify to all of our people."

It made sense. There was yet another form of suspicion within the group, directed at those who were Natives and could therefore expose the group and the existence of those with abilities at the same time. If any such individual went rogue, Norton would 'sniff' them out. I could not help wondering what would happen if Norton betrayed them, however.

"You are a naturally suspicious person, Soames. That much we know. It is why we decided to bring you in. Your work is excellent, you are thorough, but you will not accept things at face value. We expected you to try to search for the organisation. We just expected it tomorrow morning, not tonight. That kind of forward thinking is approved of, and is what will make you a great asset, should you prove yourself. You will be given your gear on the way out."

Ashley got up and moved to the glass panel, which slid open again.

"Just one thing," she added, pausing on the threshold. "If you ever use public methods to search for information on us again, it will be the last thing you do."

She walked away, leaving me to sit and take in everything that had just happened.

13

As I headed back towards the elevator, Mr Harding rejoined me and led me into a side room. A man stood behind a black counter unit and looked up as I came in. I recognised him as the one who had been modifying my laptop.

"Detective Sergeant Oliver Soames," said Harding. I wanted to tell him that I could introduce myself, but it looked like I was going to get stuck with him for a while, and antagonising a new partner did not go well. I had seen it happen before.

The man behind the desk pulled on a pair of plastic forensic gloves. He laid an identity badge case on the desk, followed by a .40-calibre pistol like the one Harding had pulled on me before, a small leather wallet, and a mobile phone. I noted that the phone was completely identical to my own.

The man held his hand out. "Phone and badge, please."

I glanced at Harding, who nodded, and I put the two items on the table, deliberately ignoring the outstretched hand. The man raised an eyebrow, but picked up my badge. He pulled the ID card from it and threw my case into a small hole in the desk. He placed the card carefully into the new case.

"Do not lose any of this equipment," he said. I took the new case from him and looked at it. It appeared no different.

"It contains a locator chip and electronic identification specific to this organisation," Harding said. "Do not lose it." He spoke the four words this second time as though I were a man being condemned to death and being told to repent. I had to struggle very hard not to hit him.

The man behind the desk then took my phone and attached what looked like a standard USB charger cable. This he then plugged into what appeared to be nothing more than a metal box which, in turn, he connected to the new phone he had pulled out. His fingers once again moved at lightning speed, darting over the new phone's keypad, and then he paused. He stared at the box for what must have been a full minute after this, until a small green light blinked from within.

He pulled the cord from my phone and inspected the phone's casing, looking at it from every conceivable angle. That done, he pulled out a small knife and a bradel. It took me a while to realise why he was mutilating a phone with a knife until I saw him push the bradel into the top right-hand corner of the new one. I knew that mark well. With dawning respect, and no small amount of curiosity, I realised that every mark or scratch on my old phone was now on the new one. He tossed my old phone down the hole.

He opened the leather wallet and I found that it contained a variety of small tools. It was a lock-picking kit, with a few extra additions. He closed the wallet again, pinned it and gave it to me.

"Don't get caught with that," he said.

"Don't." Mr Harding was clearly going to repeat every warning. I ground my teeth in frustration.

"Shoulder or belt?" asked the man.

"What?"

"Holster. Do you want a shoulder or a belt?"

"Oh. Shoulder." I had no preference really, but shoulder holsters looked cool.

"Good choice," said Harding. "Saves you buying new coats to hide it."

The man put a black shoulder holster on the unit and picked up the pistol. He put a thumb under the serial number, pulled out a pad and copied it down. He spun the pad round.

"Sign here," he said. I looked at the form, but it was just a proof-of-receipt. I signed. The man pulled out two boxes of ammunition and gave them to me. "Every round has to be accounted for. Paperwork in CID is nothing compared to what you have to fill out now. You fire that weapon, you inform us. Every round."

I held up my hand in front of Harding's face as he opened his mouth. "I got it," I said.

Harding's mouth twitched, though I could not tell what emotion that was supposed to signify. "I was going to say we're done," he said. "Put the holster on. We're going. I'll talk to you on the way home."

That sounded like a threat.

"What, no official briefing?" I asked. "No tax forms? Not even a cup of tea?"

"Wiseguy. Sign here."

We had left the room, and Harding pointed to an electronic signature pad that protruded from the wall. I looked at him for a moment, then picked up the stylus and signed. The pad immediately slid back into the wall.

"If that signature deviated more than 4% from average expected variations, you would have been rendered unconscious at which point all knowledge of this facility would have been removed from your mind - a process which does not always end well. Would you like your tax forms now?"

Harding may have been acting like a piece of work, but I registered his point. I shook my head.

"I didn't think so. Now come on. I need to talk you through procedure."

14

Terence Foxwood sat at one of the sticky, beer-caked tables of The Frog And Nettle pub nursing his third pint of the night. It had been preceded by a couple of whiskeys, and it was just beginning to take its toll. His head felt like it was bobbing along a gentle stream, the room waving slightly from side to side as it went. He put his head in his hands and groaned.

"Cheer up, mate." The unnaturally happy voice of Roger, his best friend, seemed irritating in his current state, and that was only made worse when he looked up to see two shot glasses had appeared in front of him.

"What's that? I thought you were going for a whiz," he said.

"Come on, Terry. Don't mean I can't stop at the bar on the way back now, does it?" replied Roger.

There was a point in that which had to be conceded. They threw the shots back, and Terry choked and slammed his glass back down. Roger almost missed the table, and his rolled across it and came to a stop against the pepper shaker.

"You don't get it though, Rog," said Terry, picking up where he had left off. "I mean, I felt properly old."

"Don't be ridiculous. You won't be old for another three years at least." Roger laughed uproariously at his own joke.

"I'm serious, Rog. It was like I just blacked out on the sofa. I have never had a nap during the day in my life." He said 'nap' under his breath, as if it were some great secret, or a terrible expletive.

"You probably just overdid it yesterday. I told you not to work yourself so hard. This is just a mid-life crisis, that's all."

"I went to work and spent all day sitting down."

Terry was getting annoyed by this point. He could not actually remember going to work, but he knew it was what he had to say. Rather, he recalled visiting an old friend and discussing something of great importance. It felt like it had gone well, but this afternoon it had not felt so good. He had worked a half day and gone home, but fallen asleep on the sofa. At least, he thought he had. It felt like twenty minutes had just disappeared while he was sitting on the sofa, but things like that could not happen.

"You were still working though. That's the way of it, man. That's why you don't go out with those toff friends of yours, but come down the boozer with me. S'your way of escaping from the everyday, home… um… hum-drum life."

Terry frowned at Roger. Maybe Roger's head was floating downstream faster than his. That would not do. Terry took a long pull from his pint to try to catch up. Then his phone started ringing. He ignored the first two rings and then decided to answer it. It took him a while to get his fingers into his pocket, but he managed it. He pulled out the phone and promptly dropped it on the floor.

He banged his head on the table as he leant down, and then the phone stopped ringing. He wondered whether he had imagined it ringing, and the bang on the head just made him realise it wasn't. In the darkened pub, it took him a moment to find it on the floor.

He thought about leaving it there, but decided that if his head floated any more downstream, which after the bang he felt was a serious possibility, then he might leave the phone behind. He almost dropped it again when, as his fingers grasped it, it started to ring. This time he managed to answer it.

"'Lo?" he said.

"Dad?"

"Who's this? Rachel?"

"Dad? Dad, help."

All the alcohol seemed to leech out of him as he heard the terror in his daughter's voice.

"Rachel? What's wrong?"

"Dad, Tommy's dead."

"What?"

"Tommy. He's dead, Dad. I just got home and he wasn't in. He's lying out on the back lawn. Our axe is stuck in him and there's blood everywhe-"

Rachel broke down into sobs on the other end of the line.

15

I managed to grab a total of about four hours sleep before my new phone rang. I rolled over and onto the book I had been reading the night before - Dickens' *David Copperfield*. Usually I found pleasure in reading, but I guess I had been too tired.

"Time to get up."

"Harding." I turned my head away from the phone and cursed, then sighed and turned back to speak to him. "You need to work on your bedside manner."

"I'm on my way to pick you up, Soames. There in fifteen." The line clicked and I shut the phone.

A cursory shower and a slice of toast was all I managed before Harding banged on the door. I almost tripped over my trouser leg as I yanked clothes on on the way to open it. Harding looked down at my hands fumbling with my belt and then took in the mess my flat was in. I had not had time to clear anything up after he and his men had burst in to stop my internet search. Fortunately, the door had been repaired while I was out.

"You might want to take that." Harding pointed at my new holster. I strapped it on and picked up a second slice of toast.

"Let's go," I said.

On the way down to the car, Harding briefed me on the situation. I became more incredulous as I listened to him. It seemed almost ridiculous that we should be called out on something like this, but I gave him his time, and did not interrupt until he paused for breath.

"Okay, now hang on a minute," I said. "We are being called out because someone killed this guy's dog?"

Harding gave me a scathing look. "No. We are being called out because someone killed this guy's dog and he has a blank of some twenty minutes that he cannot explain. He said that he fell asleep on the sofa, but he did not believe it himself, never mind what I thought. Mr Foxwood called your boys at half past two this morning, and it has filtered through to us. Took its bloody time, though." This last statement was said mostly to himself, and said a lot to me about what he thought about the police.

"What time is it now?" I asked. I had not had time to drink any coffee and my mind was not happy with that fact.

"Twenty to six," replied Harding.

"Great." I sighed. "So what are we dealing with? I assumed that I was going to be assigned to the Wattler case, but now you're sending me off to something completely different?"

"When there is only one case, we keep a new recruit on it. Should there be a second, it is always preferable to put the newbie onto that one. That way, you can enter a case with eyes opened to what could be going on. If you get the first case, you have already got ideas as to what happened before you even join us, and those can be difficult to break."

"I guess that makes sense." I checked my holster for about the fiftieth time.

"You might not want to let anyone see that. It makes your lot uneasy if they see someone flashing one of their badges, but carrying a non-regulation firearm."

"Thanks." I hated to admit it, but Harding had a point. "So there is someone... special involved in this then?"

"That is yet to be determined. It could be that we turn up to the address and come right back home. Then you will get the Wattler case back again. Until we know for sure, however, we have to assume that our involvement will be needed. Since no-one knows we exist to call, we have to preempt the necessity once we hear about a case. Do you remember what we discussed last night?"

"Yes. We are regular policemen but with additional jurisdiction to combat assault or manipulation from person or persons unknown with abilities outside the recognised norm."

"Don't parrot." Harding made a face like he had just stepped in something. "That does not show understanding - just an ability to absorb rhetoric."

"I am the same man I was yesterday." I tried not to bridle as I spoke. "I behave the same way, abide by the same rules, and have additional recognition only with other members of the MSCE. I can act differently only if something weird threatens me or any civilian. Until that time, I just assume that all of the knowledge you forced into my head yesterday is absolutely, perfectly everyday, and that nothing has changed in the last twenty-four hours. If someone asks a difficult question, I refer them to you or the Quack." I caught myself. "I mean, DCS Kwaku."

"Your tone is unnecessary, but the facts are correct."

"What are you, some kind of robot?"

Harding looked at me, and for a second I felt like he was about to stop the car and have me thrown out. Then he looked away and out of the window.

"I was brought up in complicated circumstances," he said. "I do not have the social skills required to interact in a manner deemed proper by society."

"But what about yesterday? In the office? You seemed almost kind for a moment."

"I am having... treatment."

I waited for anything else, but he just kept staring out of the window. I tried to talk to the driver, but he did not reply. I sat there for ten minutes, feeling more awkward than I ever had in my life.

"So how do we know if this is a case for us?" I asked, eventually. "When do we know?"

"He'll know soon enough," replied Harding.

I opened my mouth to ask who, and then realised I already knew. "Norton."

The silence returned for a couple of minutes, and then I realised something was bothering me, and I turned once again to see Harding staring straight ahead with those hard eyes.

"You keep saying 'your lot' when referring to the police. Are you not in the force?"

"No."

"Who do you work for, then?"

"I used to work for MI-5."

16

Having followed innumerable backroads, we arrived at the Foxwood household at five minutes to eight. The dawn chorus had presumably given up and gone back to bed, which is precisely what I wanted to do. However, I pulled myself out of the car and walked up to the door of yet another ridiculously big house, with bay windows in the front room and an ostentatious porch. It differed wildly from the houses around it, which I guessed the neighbours were none too happy about.

Harding waved his badge at the constable guarding the door and walked in, so I followed suit. We were three steps into the house when Norton came out of another door and turned towards us. He gestured that we should go and talk to him before entering further. When we were within a couple of paces of him, he spoke in a low voice. "No-one close. We can talk."

"Report," said Harding.

"Dog is in the garden. Daughter is upstairs staring at the ceiling. Father is in the conservatory, over that way." Norton pointed towards the back of the house. "Oh, one other thing. Same perp as the happy couple."

"What?" I asked.

"Whoever did whatever they did to whatever their names were also did it to the father here."

"The Wattlers, Norton. A little respect, please?" Norton's flippancy had annoyed me, and I did not think respect too much to ask. I was known as stuffy around the station for expecting the same of my constables, but morgue humour did nothing for me.

"Oh, sorry." Norton's eyes laughed as he said it. "I'm off to check for forced entry." He winked at me as he walked away. I remembered the same statement from him at the Wattlers'. He wasn't as much of a fool as I had thought then, clearly. I wondered whether it might be code for him going to do MSCE-type things rather than basic investigation.

"Your play then, Soames. You want the father while I take the daughter?" asked Harding. The very idea of him bludgeoning the poor girl with that steel club of an attitude made me wince.

"No, I think we'll take the father together," I said.

He nodded and followed me through to the conservatory. The man at the table, resting his chin in his hands, made me think of that moment when tomato ketchup is about to pour from a glass bottle. He looked like he was just barely hanging on, and at any moment would collapse onto the floor. His eyes were red, and tear-marks stained his cheeks, hands and wrists.

"Mr Foxwood," I said. "My name is Detective Sergeant Soames, and this is my colleague…" I was flipping open my badge when I suddenly realised that I did not know Harding's rank.

Harding flipped his badge next to mine. "Inspector Harding."

"I have told the officers everything I know. Why won't you people leave me alone?" The voice was small, coming from such a large man.

"I am sorry, Mr Foxwood," I said. "It is a matter of routine, but we will only ask a couple of questions and then look around."

Foxwood waved a hand with a sigh.

"Can you tell us whether you met anyone in the last couple of days who might have had a reason to want to do you harm?"

Foxwood looked genuinely surprised at that, and sat up.

"What on earth has that to do with anything?" he asked. "I killed him. I killed Tommy. I killed him." He broke into renewed sobbing. Spouting stuff like that, I wondered how he was not in handcuffs and in the back of a police car, but I assumed Norton had stopped it.

"Sir, we understand that you believe this to be the case, but you had a blackout, correct? It is possible that a similar blackout happened to someone else, and the coincidence needs to be investigated."

Harding glared at me, as if I was giving away too much. I ignored him. Foxwood would not remember a thing by this evening. Judging by the smell coming from his clothes, he would be raising more than just one glass in Tommy's memory.

"What, you think someone slipped me a drug or something? I have only seen people from work and my friend Roger in the last couple of days. I tipped a guy's pint last night, but I don't suppose you think he drugged me, or broke into my house, knocked me on the head and killed my dog…"

"No, sir, thank you."

I raised placating hands, and Foxwood grunted and looked away. I walked out of the door of the conservatory and into the garden. The first thing that struck me was that it was huge. It tapered towards the end, but it was long and well-populated with varieties of plants. Foxwood could clearly afford a gardener. He did not strike me as the green-fingered type.

The second thing I noticed was the blue sheet covering a patch of grass. I went around to the far side, so that I would not show what was underneath to the men in the house, and lifted it. The sheet covered an enormous splash of red only ten feet or so from the house, in the centre of which lay the dead dog, badly mutilated, a hand axe protruding from its head at an angle. The grass all around it was stained in more splashes or specks of blood. It was not as horrific as the twin murder, but somehow it hurt more to look at.

As I went back in, Foxwood was sobbing again. I looked at Harding, who rolled his eyes. A quick canvas of the room showed no evidence of a break-in. I was thinking I should look at the living room sofa where Foxwood had supposedly fallen asleep when I caught sight of his phone. I said out loud that I was going to take the number, but my only reply was the soft sniffling.

I picked it up and turned it on. It was not password protected. I checked the settings for the handset's number and copied it down. We could trace phone records, just in case. Given that Harding seemed to be determined to leave me entirely on my own, I did not really know what I was looking for, and so I just did the job I would normally do.

I turned back and moved to leave, convinced that Foxwood would not be able to explain what had happened any more than I could.

"Wait," he said, as I reached the door. "There was one other person. I… I've just started having therapy. I visited my psychiatrist the day before yesterday."

I gestured a constable to bring Foxwood in to the station, and then left. I had a feeling Mr Foxwood would be making a few more urgent visits to the shrink over the next couple of weeks.

17

"So what do you think?" I asked Harding, once we were back in the car with Norton.

"About what?"

"Who is this guy? What can he do? You have experience with this that I don't."

Harding shrugged. "Too early to say. It could be anything. Extreme post-hypnotic suggestion, mind control, possibly even something we've never heard of."

"Okay, so method needs to wait. In that case, what about motive? Let's look into his rationale and try to work out what this guy's objective is, or what kind of man he is."

"It's possible that he's just a serial killer."

"Yes, but we need to cross-reference the victims and find out whether they had a connection. Besides, a serial killer who kills a married couple and then a dog? Where's the logic?"

"Who are the victims?"

I stopped at that for just a second. I wanted to say 'everyone', but I knew that would only earn me a smart answer. Harding's question was one of objective intent. Who was this crime meant to hurt the most. "Well I hardly suspect that whoever this is took control of someone to kill a dog. It must be the people who suffered the blackouts."

"A valid suggestion, but you are assuming that this is some form of mind control."

"There was no footprint in the house this time," said Norton. "Of course, it is entirely possible that whoever it was could have stood outside."

"It was a mistake last time," I said. "They were more careful."

"Or it was unrelated. The footprint at the Wattlers' was left by one of them after they had been gardening. Or the attacker wasn't there this time."

I sighed. "It's bad enough examining a crime scene normally. At least then everything is pertinent. Here, it is impossible to know whether something is relevant or not."

"No," said Harding. "Everything is still pertinent. Don't forget, this is just another crime scene. The footprint could have been from an onlooker, a participant, the actual killer or someone throwing a dirty boot across the room. Don't think any differently because of all this. Just be more open to possibility."

"Okay, let's work this through," I said. "Possible scenario. The killer is like Creeker. He has to touch his victim to control them. Hence the footprint in the Wattler house. He gets into the house and grabs his victim and chaperones him into each death." Even as I said it, I realised that this was a really unnerving prospect.

"Which means the victims knew the killer," said Norton.

"Why?"

"No forced entry." There was a slight smirk on Norton's face as he said it.

"But then what about the wife?"

"What about her," asked Harding.

"She was almost naked. She would have covered up if her husband was there with someone else."

"Unless someone else was already there."

"Why do you say that?"

"Mrs Rhodes. She didn't see anyone get out of Wattler's car. She just saw the door left open"

Harding could be irritatingly astute sometimes.

"Affair, then?" I asked.

"Possible. No reports of a regular male visitor from anyone though."

"Yet."

Harding waved a hand in concession.

"Could be a lesbian affair," Norton added. "Did we check regular female visitors?"

"Are you serious?" I asked.

"Yes." He was, too. I could tell. "Or it could have been a female friend over discussing dresses."

"Where are we going, by the way?" I asked, trying to move away from the realm of rampant speculation.

"The station," replied Harding. "Normal day, remember?"

"Of course. Will Kwaku be there?"

"Who is to say? He had a press conference scheduled for this morning, covering the Wattler case. He may have arranged to delay that as a result of this mess. Did you report the connection?"

This last was to Norton, who nodded. "Yes."

"Then he may also wait to see how far the rabbit-hole goes. The last thing we need is the public panicking about a serial killer, and having him get away with it in the chaos.

"Who kills a dog?" said Norton. I looked back, but he was staring out the window.

We drove on in silence. It was not a long journey, but it seemed to be crawling by. I was itching to work out what was going on. It was bad enough knowing that the possibilities were so extreme that we might never catch this guy. It was worse not knowing which one of the possibilities was the actual cause.

Who kills a dog? Thinking about it, that was actually a very good question.

18

Searching through the victims' records proved to be frustratingly slow. With the addition of all the possible complications, every single detail needed to be examined, and the solution might not be immediately apparent, even once we saw it. I was not sure regular police logic applied any more. How could an answer be defined as simple when you had potential mind control involved?

I liked the detective work. It was better than filling out paperwork and interested me more than being out on the street. However, whoever this was had apparently killed two people and a dog, and might well go for more. I was anxious to get him. Serial killers provided both the best cause for detective work and the greatest pressure.

So, I sat at my desk and trawled through records like an auditor, but instead of checking that everything matched up, I was looking for the one thing that did not.

Benjamin Wattler, age 35. A moderately successful business lawyer who was somewhere above the middle of the pack when it came to proficiency, judging by his cases, and somewhat better at charlatanism, judging by his inflated reputation. Worked for Hampton and Proust law firm since he had been called to the bar nine years ago.

He had not, as far as I could tell, dealt with a case involving Terry Foxwood. His record was clean. Excellent bank credit, with substantial holdings. Member of local golf and boxing clubs. He had been a scholar at his secondary school - private - and by all indications was a very academic, studious person. There was nothing to raise alarm bells with him until I looked under known criminals for any associations.

Marvin Stoller. A petty criminal with a habit for minor theft, but with one charge for Grievous Bodily Harm. It had gone to court, and Stoller had been given a sentence of five years, a slightly shortened term on the grounds that he had been provoked and had demonstrated remorse. He had served three and a half and was granted parole after that. He had completed that parole seven years ago. I flagged Stoller as someone to look at. He went to the same boxing club as Wattler, but did not seem to have any reason to wish harm on the man.

Terry Foxwood, age 34. Owned a small storage supply company that had been responsible for council contracts as well as a couple of significant private ones. The work had allowed him to expand the business a little, though not enough to own the kind of property he did. The explanation of this was further down. One DUI charge, eight years ago. He had sued for wrongful arrest and been awarded a substantial, and suspiciously large, sum for loss of business and various other reasons.

I frowned at that, and made a mental note to ask him about it and look into it in greater detail. Went to a local state school where he was also academic, although his true success appeared to have been in art. Apparently a member of a local amateur dramatic society. Regular drinker, and founder of the Real Ale Recognition Society. That rather impressed me until I glanced at its member list.

Marvin Stoller's name was on it.

It was not much to go on, and there was no obvious motive for Stoller to want to hurt either of them, but it was the only connection I could find between the two men. Perhaps the thing that matched was going to be the key point after all.

My next port of call was the archive room. I ran through the register to see if I could find Stoller's name, but it was not there. Either he was not our guy, or he had not yet been uncovered as an individual possessing an ability.

On a random impulse, I looked up details of Stoller's GBH trial. There was nothing particularly untoward about it. As far as I could see, everything happened by the book. The victim was not associated with either of the two we were investigating, either at the time of his trial or since, and the case had simply run its course.

I browsed through the associated press material to see what was there. The case had garnered some local attention, and various newspapers and TV news stations had reported it. Stoller did not come across as a career criminal, or someone who would aspire to become a serial killer at any point, but that did not mean anything. People could just suddenly snap.

I was about to give up when I scanned the final news article, from after Stoller's release, and stopped dead in my tracks. I went back to the top and read it properly. Much of it was Stoller complaining that he had lost time with his kid and so on. He maintained that he had been provoked into the assault, and that he was remorseful for his conduct. However, it was the paragraph following that which caught my eye:

> Mr Stoller then went on to blame the fact that he had been imprisoned on a weakly-mounted defence. He claimed that he had asked a good friend, who we may not name, to represent him, despite the fact that the friend's specialisation was not in criminal law, but that this friend had declined to do so. Mr Stoller said that he would be seeking renumeration or "some other way for amends to be made" for his time in jail.

I re-read the passage several times, and the more I did, the more it seemed like the journalist was simply trying to add a little spice to an otherwise rather mundane story with her quote. However, one thought kept digging away at my mind.

What if the friend Stoller had been talking about was Ben Wattler? What if he had asked Wattler to defend him, and Wattler had put him off? To Stoller's mind, was it possible that Wattler had dismissed a friend to the care and protection of a lesser lawyer? If so, could Stoller be riled up enough to seek vengeance years later?

This did not explain the attack on Foxwood's dog, but it was the best shot at a motive that I had so far.

19

Marvin Stoller was not the easiest man to find. No-one had heard of him at his last known address, but it was a rough estate, so that did not surprise me. People came and went from that estate with disturbing regularity. However, we managed to track him down through a phone call with his brother, Edgar, who had taken care of him after he got out of jail.

Marvin had spent a lot of time at Edgar's place since, for his brother had taken him in whenever he could no longer afford his own rent. Finally he had thrown him out not two months earlier, and Marvin could now be found living with a girl who supported both of them with a job as a stripper in a disreputable club, and presumably a side-line career garnered from her club clientele. Edgar had not heard from him in three weeks, and knew nothing about the girl. He just had an address, and we had to check housing records to identify the girl.

The flat was on a council estate in the middle of nowhere, at least as far as shopping and anything interesting went. The building was a hideous lovechild of the 1980s and bad architecture. It was an obvious place to find someone living off a pittance, and the graffiti and litter surrounding it did not speak of a pleasant or hygienic environment. Harding positively turned his nose up as we approached the building, and I have to confess that I had a momentary sinking feeling at the prospect of going in.

As we arrived, two patrol cars and an armed response unit joined us, called in by Harding. There was absolutely no way of knowing what this guy was capable of, and it seemed that the MSCE did not take chances. I cannot say that I was complaining about that. The officers spread out to cover us and the ARU team leader nodded to Harding when they were ready.

We walked up to the door and pressed the doorbell. There was no obvious noise. I waited a moment, held my ear to the door and depressed the bell again. Nothing happened. I rolled my eyes at Harding and then banged on the door. Still nothing. I banged again and shouted: "Police, open up." A pause. "Freddie Gold? Open the door, or we'll do it for you." I banged again.

"This is pointless," said Harding, and pushed me to one side. He pulled back his foot and I just managed to stop him from launching himself forwards as the door began to unlatch. He fell to the ground, cursing.

A girl opened the door. The first thing I noticed was the bags under her eyes and the haggard expression. Assuming this was Freddie Gold, her file said she was twenty-seven, but she could easily pass for thirty-five.

It was not my first time seeing a working girl out of her get-up, but it never ceased to surprise me when I did. She showed worry lines and a pallid complexion that only emphasised how much older than her age she looked. Her figure looked to be pleasing enough, although it was disguised beneath a baggy sweater that was several sizes too large. A cigarette rested between her lips, which were cracked and dry.

"Freddie Gold?" I asked.

"Ruby," she said.

"I apologise, miss. I'm looking for Freddie Gold."

She took the cigarette from her mouth and blew smoke at me. Menthol. "No, Ruby. I don't like that first name."

"Freddie?"

"Short for Frederica. You work it out. You the police? Better come in then."

She opened the door wide, and I walked in. Harding, dusting himself off, followed me in and moved away to look around the flat.

"My name is Detective Sergeant Soames, and that is Detective Inspector Harding. We're looking for Marvin Stoller, Ruby. Is he here?"

"Marv? Why?"

"Is he here, Ruby? You could be in danger."

"Marv ain't been here for a week."

Her accent was a thick London street drone, mostly monotone, and she had the typical lazy pronunciation that went with it, half of the letters in a word missing or swallowed. Her voice itself was tired and worn, and she croaked a little.

"We have information that he has been living with you for the past two months," said Harding.

"Yeah, that's true, but he ain't here now. What you want him for?"

"Ruby, we are simply conducting an investigation and wanted to ask Mr Stoller some questions relating to it," I explained. "It is possible that he may have information vital to our inquiries."

"You think that he done something, don't you?"

I raised an eyebrow. "Why do you ask that?"

"This ain't the nicest place. You lot are always here, and I've been asked a lotta questions about a lotta people. It gets so you know when it's concern and when it's suspicion, and you two are suspicious. Especially him."

She nodded at Harding, who had just come back in from canvassing the flat, and hopefully calling off the ARU before too many people had come out to look. I stifled a snort, but raised an eyebrow towards him in a questioning gesture. He shook his head. The girl was alone.

"It's too early to accuse anyone of anything," I said, trying to reassure her. "We just want to speak to Marvin. That's all. Please, can you tell us where he is?"

"We will take you in for obstruction of an official investigation if you don't," added Harding. I shot him a look. We could not afford to alienate Ruby as a possible witness. She was our only lead at this point.

"But we don't want to do that," I said hastily.

"Okay, keep your hair on. I'll tell you." Ruby went to a pile of papers and flicked through them. She held out a business card. "Try here."

I looked at the card. It had a name, address, phone number and an e-mail address. It was a local address, not ten minutes from here, and the e-mail was erin.ames@axc.org.uk. It meant nothing to me. I flipped the card over. It was a business card for Ames Xander Cremations. I looked up at Ruby.

"Yeah," she said. "Marv's dead."

20

"When did you last see Marvin?" I asked.

"Tuesday night." It was Wednesday.

"Last week, I assume?"

"Yeah. He took an overdose. Something about owing too much to three different dealers. He were just looking for a bit of a blank night, you know? I were a bit gone myself, and I didn't realise he was so wasted. Shame. He were a nice guy, in his own way. Never tried to take advantage. Never looked at me wrong, you know what I mean?"

I felt a little sad to think that her definition of nice was probably anyone who did not try and force their way into her knickers within half an hour of knowing her. Underneath an outer layer of bad experiences, rough atmosphere and jaded personality lurked, I suspected, a rather pretty girl. I assumed her figure helped her get a few tips. It probably also caught the attention of the wrong kind of man, a lot of the time.

The women I saw were respectable in the presentation of their business, and had the right to refuse to enter a room or building if they wished. Ruby probably did not have that right either at work or elsewhere. It was the only way she could afford her rent and, in this area, she would probably get roughed up if she refused.

"Did Marvin have a job?" asked Harding. It was not where I had intended to take the questioning.

"No," said Ruby. "He had one before he left his brother's, but he didn't have anything here. I don't know why he left his last place. It would have been a trek from here, but not too long."

From what Edgar had said on the phone, I suspected Marvin had been fired. 'Lethargic, good-for-nothing layabout' seemed to have been the kindest phrase Edgar could bring to mind.

"So how did he afford his habit?"

"He didn't. Not really. He had a little cash and bought the first few hits with that when he got here. Then he stole from me. He thought I didn't know, but I saw him the second time. I were going to talk to him, but then he vanished for a couple of days. I thought he had gone back to his brother, so I left it."

"Then he come back. I started to question him, but he had lost it. Before he went wherever, he were high half the time. The rest he just went out walking. I followed him once to see where he went. He just walked for ages. After he got back, he were never off the stuff. I don't know what he took at any point. Seemed to be whatever he could score. He were troubled, Marv."

"Why did you let him stay?"

Ruby looked uncomfortable. She fidgeted a little with her hands.

"You were lonely," I said. She nodded. "Your only company was men who did not care for you or appreciate you for anything other than a means to their own gratification."

A tear ran down her cheek and she hid her head. At that moment, despite my own choices and needs, I wanted to take her for the best dinner I could afford, pay for her time, and send her home. I wanted just to show her one night of friendship and entertainment, without the intrusive calling of sex. She looked like she could have been the loneliest girl in the world.

"How did you afford the cremation?" I asked, getting back on track.

"I didn't."

"Then who paid for it?"

"Who else?" she replied. "His brother."

21

We asked a few more questions, but it was not long before Harding and I were back in our car, the ARU was re-routed, and everyone was heading to Edgar Stoller's house.

"I can't believe he suckered us," I said. Harding did not reply. "Is he the murderer? He did not seem the type on the phone."

"I'm not sure your 'types' count for much any more, Sergeant," said Harding. "Besides, how can you tell without meeting someone."

"I give you the second point, but I disagree on the first. Power corrupts. That much is a fact. The deciding factor is how corruptible a person is, and how they choose to deal with corruption. I can see Stoller committing some crimes, but not murder. Call it base instinct."

"We should have brought Norton."

"Sniffer would have helped, yes, but neither you nor I expected another party in the mix. Anyway, he had to go back to the Penthouse."

"Sniffer?" Harding's lips cracked into a smirk. "I hadn't thought of that."

"It's what the force calls him."

Harding did not reply.

"How do you think this sounds then? Marvin is screwed over by his friend, Ben Wattler, at least in his eyes. Something happens to get him out of sorts with Foxwood. Naturally his brother only hears Marvin's side of it and does what any brother would do - sets out to protect his sibling. Only Edgar has powers, and he uses them thinking that he can get revenge without anyone ever catching him?"

"That is pure speculation, Sergeant," said Harding.

"Of course it bloody is, but play with this a little, won't you?" I needed something of the old life to hang onto, and Harding was really not helping just now.

"No, actually, I won't. I have been in this game now for almost ten years." He put a lot of sarcasm into the word game. "If there is one thing that I have learned since then, it is that forming an opinion before you know all the facts can kill you more quickly than charging into a hostile situation without a flak jacket."

"Fair enough. But do you at least admit that the idea is credible?"

"Yes. It is that, at least. However, we do not know Edgar's ability. We are also still using guesswork to blame him in the first place. We have no evidence to suggest that the killer is him."

"No, but we have admittedly tenuous grounds for an arrest under obstruction of justice, which will at least give us time."

Harding nodded, and waved a hand dismissively.

"It's your investigation," he said. "I am only here to offer advice and to keep you out of trouble."

I somehow doubted that was true, but I took what I got and shut up for the rest of the journey. We pulled up to Edgar's house - yet another ostentatious building, but much more tastefully so, this time.

"Seems that however much Edgar protects his brother, he doesn't help him," Harding said. I had to agree with that. For someone to afford this and yet throw his brother out seemed cold.

We approached the door, once again supported by other officers, and Harding hammered on it. I pointed at the doorbell, but he gave me a withering look. This time, he was just raising his arm to bang a second time when we heard footsteps behind the door. He stood back and the door was opened by a tall, thin man wearing round spectacles and an expression of resignation.

"Detectives. Harding and Soames, I presume?" he said. I had given our names when I called.

"Yes. Edgar Stoller?"

The tall man nodded and opened the door, gesturing for us to come in. A suitcase, facing away from us, was sitting open in the hallway, and there was a small pile of books on the ground next to it. Stoller was preparing to run. I stepped forwards and saw, out of the corner of my eye, Harding slip a hand surreptitiously into his jacket to take hold of his gun.

I went to pull my handcuffs from my belt, but Stoller held a hand up. I read acceptance in the gesture and stopped. Harding tensed, but Stoller just nodded, picked up his keys and locked the door behind him.

"Edgar Stoller," I said. "I am arresting you for obstruction of justice during the course of a murder investigation. You do not have to say anything, but it may harm your defence if you do not mention, when questioned, something which you later rely on in court. Anything you do say may be given in evidence."

I gestured to one of the nearby police officers to cuff Edgar Stoller and put him in a car to go to the police station – acceptance or not, we would not take chances, and I could not help noticing that while 'obstruction of justice' had gained no reaction, when I had taken the gamble and mentioned murder, his eyes had widened and he started to shake.

22

"Officers present are Detective Sergeant Soames and Detective Inspector Harding. The time is three forty two P.M." I finished introducing the interview for the recording and sat back to let Harding lead.

"Mr Stoller, at ten minutes to eleven this morning, you gave us a location for your brother, Marvin," he said. "You did this in the full knowledge that your brother was dead, having paid for his cremation with your own funds. Can you please explain why you did this?"

I noticed immediately increased signs of discomfort in Stoller. His eye movement quickened, and he refused to meet Harding's gaze. I expected him to start sweating at any moment. I would have started more softly, but it was not up to me.

"I… I don't know," replied Stoller.

"You don't know why you deliberately lied to a police detective and obstructed the course of a murder investigation?"

"I don't know anything about a murder. Who has been murdered? Not Marvin. He died of an overdose. Ruby told me. I saw the body. I saw the pills."

"Mr Stoller," I said, before Harding could attack again. "No-one is accusing you of murder, or doubting the fact that Marvin committed suicide. We may not have the remains to examine, but it certainly fits with his self-destructive personality and troubled past. Forgive me, but may I ask whether there were more misdemeanours than were reported to the police?"

Stoller looked sheepish for a moment, and then nodded. "Yes. Marvin got away with a couple of thefts, and I managed to smooth over a couple of instances where he tried to rough up some guys."

"Your brother was a sad, troubled man, who was trying to find a little happiness in this life, and unfortunately he only found it in substance abuse that harmed him. Harmed others too, no doubt - especially you. It is obvious that you were extremely loyal to your brother, and that you loved him very much despite his failings."

"I do. I did," said Stoller. I could see tears welling up in his eyes, but he did not let himself cry. "I did everything for him. Except tell him that I loved him."

"He knew," I said. "You may not have said it, but he knew."

Stoller smiled a half-smile. "I'm not sure I believe that, Detective Sergeant, but thank you."

"So why were you protecting him this time? Why, now he is dead, did you feel you had to protect your brother once again?"

"I didn't," he said, and took a deep breath. "I was protecting myself. I was worried that it would get out that I helped him violate his parole."

"How did you do that?"

"I gave him the money he used to buy his first lot of drugs when he was still on parole. I even went with him. It was nothing much. Mostly weed, and a little cocaine. I thought that if I supervised his habit, he might be able to start fighting it. That's what he really needed, you know? He needed to be weaned off. I couldn't cold turkey him. I couldn't go through that. I did the same thing again this time."

"Why did you not send him to a rehab clinic?" asked Harding.

"He went once of his own accord. He really didn't get on with that life. He told me he left because it made him want to commit suicide."

I knew nothing about rehabilitation, and so I let that go, though I had a hunch that a lot of heavy users felt like that as the withdrawal really kicked in. Either way, it seemed to me like his brother should have been in rehab, and not living under the imperfect supervision of someone who did not know what he was doing.

"So you went with your brother to buy drugs both times since he left your house two months ago?" asked Harding.

"No, just the first time. I don't know where he got the money for the second run, but it wasn't from me. I didn't know he had gone again until Freddie called me to say he was dead. He must have gone more often too - he couldn't have made it on just two buys - but I don't know about any others."

"He stole the money from Ruby. Freddie."

"Oh. Oh, I suppose I should have guessed. Oh, Marvin…"

"Who was the dealer?" I asked.

"He went to different people each time. Said it became a habit while he was on parole. Hoped that if he were discovered, any one dealer could vouch that he had only been once, and he might get some leniency. I don't suppose that would have worked."

"Why did you send him to Freddie? Her lifestyle doesn't seem the kind of thing he should be surrounded by."

"I didn't. I… I told him to get out. I said that it was not working out, having him in the house, and that he needed to leave me alone for a while. I only meant a couple of hours. I just wanted him to go for a walk. I was upset because he had broken a vase that belonged to our grandmother. It was all I had left of her. I stormed out to clear my head, went to buy a newspaper and by the time I got back he had gone. He left a note with a forwarding address and asked that I not contact him."

"Was that unusual behaviour for Marvin?"

"No. I wish I could say it was, but he had his own network of 'friends'. I use the term loosely. If he wanted to get away, he would go to one of them. That's what he did this time, I guess. Who was this Freddie or whatever her name is? She rented the place he was at? Is she as bad as he was?"

"No, she's not. She rents the place, yes, and she is an exotic dancer and occasional escort," I said. There was no way to temper that fact with Stoller in his current mood.

"Oh," he said. His face fell.

"Had he mentioned her before?"

"No. At least, I don't think so. He spoke about a lot of people, but I never knew who they were. They were just other facets of his life as far as I was concerned. He did not go into any of his personal life that I could not see for myself."

"Mr Stoller, I think we have all we need for the moment. DI Harding and I are going to go and look over some notes on the case. I'll have a constable bring you some coffee and you can sit here for a while. This must be a difficult time for you, and we're sorry for your loss. DS Soames and DI Harding are leaving the room. Interview postponed at three fifty nine P.M."

Harding glared at me, but followed me out. As soon as the door closed, he rounded on me.

"What's that about, Sergeant?"

"It's not him, Harding. You must be able to see that as well as I." I was angry and upset by the plight of both of the Stollers, but particularly the mess that Marvin had left his brother in.

"I see one thing and know another. We still do not know whether he has an ability. If he does, this could all be a cover story, but you're treating him too much like a victim."

"And he would be right to do so, Harding." Norton came round the corner. "Got back a few moments ago and wandered past to see who you had. This guy is as regular as Soames here."

"See? You need to trust a policeman's instinct, Harding. I know what I am talking about."

"Fine then, but that leaves us with an even bigger problem," said Harding. "Our murderer is still out there."

23

"So let me understand," I said to Norton, a few minutes later. "How does your ability work?"

"You ever had someone walk by you who you know well and who always wears a specific scent?" he replied.

"Yeah, sure."

"Well it's kind of like that, but it's not a literal scent - I just use that word to describe it. Every ability gives off a specific scent to me. I could smell the same scent at both crime scenes, and so I know it's the same guy." He surrounded the word 'smell' with air quotes.

"Why do you say guy?"

"Honestly? In terms you can understand, it smells like a guy. You don't expect a lady to walk past you wearing Calvin Klein's MAN. But sometimes it can happen, so I'm just guessing, really."

"Okay, so can you follow the trail?"

"No. The scent fades the same way perfume does. The only difference is that it hangs around where the ability is actually used. The killer's house would reek of it if he used it in the last day or two. The victims' houses did also, because the effects of the skill manifested there. Otherwise, you might as well ask me to tell you what perfume the girl you met last night was wearing. If it's not on you, I can't."

"Fair enough. Good, old-fashioned detective work it is, then."

"Looks that way." He smiled and left. Now that I understood Norton's ability better, and had gained a better knowledge of him as a person, I realised that I liked the guy. He was an uncomplicated human being who did not apologise for himself and was actually remarkably happy with his lot. He just played very well at being the slightly awkward man I thought I had known before.

I turned my mind to the case. 'Good, old-fashioned detective work' could take many forms. However, I was making the assumption that forensics would only take us so far in this case. Norton's ability was the only tool we could trust at this point. I decided that I had to interview Terence Foxwood. He had to know something. I was putting my thoughts together when Harry came in.

"You never made it to the pub last night," he said. His tone was a little accusing.

"Sorry. Late one. Lots to think about with this case."

"Don't you mean cases?" He emphasised the plural. "I heard you picked up a second. They can't be linked from what I've heard."

"No, it seems unlikely."

"What do you mean, 'unlikely'? One guy is killed by some bloke, seemingly after seeing his wife butchered in front of him. That sounds pretty cut-and-dried, apart from knowing who the perp is. The other goes schizo and kills his daughter's dog and then pretends he knows nothing about it, or he gets trauma-induced amnesia or something. The bad guy is pretty clear in that scenario."

Oh, if only you knew, Harry. "That's true, but I need to interrogate the suspect in the canicide case."

"The what? The canicide? Is that even a word?"

"I don't know, Harry. It just sounds right, okay?"

"Fine, man, jeez. I didn't mean to prick a nerve."

"That's okay." I flopped back in my chair. "Sorry. I'm just tired. I…"

I discovered yesterday that there is a secret branch of the Metropolitan Police Service working in amongst us that involves itself clandestinely in cases where the perpetrators are people with the ability to do things that you and, up until yesterday, I would not deem possible. I was taken to their headquarters and am now a member, and those cases you are talking about were actually the result of one man who can make people kill other people without even being there. Possibly.

"I had a bad night," I said.

"That's okay man. Happens to the best of us. You drinking tonight, at least?"

"No, I don't think so. I need to interview this suspect and I will have to give Kwaku reports after that."

"Hang on a minute. I'm the Detective Inspector here. Since when did you stop reporting to me?"

"Ask the Quack." I did not want to have to find my way out of that one. "He asked for it specifically in this case."

"No, that's okay. I don't need to get chewed out for insubordination. The only reason I look good in this place is because I get to report all your cases."

"Come on, Harry," I laughed. "You know that's not true."

"Yep," he said. "But you're smiling again." He left.

I just wondered if I would be smiling after my interview with Terence Foxwood.

24

Foxwood had managed to calm down a little by this point, but he was still agitated. I asked Harding to watch this interview from the observation room and said that I wanted Norton in with me. I did not trust Harding not to spook Foxwood into an emotional hole that he would not be able to get back out of in a hurry. Harding raised an eyebrow - just another way of making him appear sinister - but acquiesced. It seemed I really did have the run of the investigation.

Norton and I sat down with Foxwood and I announced us for the tape. I thought that Foxwood seemed pleased not to see Harding, but it was difficult to say.

"Mr Foxwood," I began. "I'm sorry about what you have been through, but I'm afraid that I must ask you to tell us all the details from the beginning."

"When I blacked out you mean?"

"Just before that, if you would. Anything from earlier in the day that might have triggered this black-out?"

"No. I had not drunk a thing by that point, and I honestly could not say what caused it. I was in work in the morning."

"What do you do?"

"I am a business owner, Sergeant. I run a supply business. We make boxes. It may not sound like much, but my company recently revolutionised a way of making small, strong boxes with less cardboard. We could save millions of trees. We started shipping trials about six months ago, had a few problems, fixed the product and we are preparing a major press conference in three weeks time to unveil the design for business use. I filed the patent on it myself, and it could turn my company into a major player."

"Very well, Mr Foxwood," I said. "Have you experienced any additional stress at all over the last few weeks? Either at work or at home?" Like a death-threat to your family, I wanted to add.

"No, not really. There is the press conference about the new design, and that is taking up a lot of my time, but I have people working for me on that."

"And at home?"

"No. Nothing really. Not until this all happened. My daughter was doing so well at school - she leaves this summer, and is in good stead to go to Cambridge. At least, she was." Foxwood's shoulders slumped.

"Okay. So you were in work in the morning." I gestured for him to continue.

"Well, I was working a half day. I had decided that I could do with spending an evening with Rachel, my daughter. I haven't seen enough of her lately. Do you have children, Sergeant?"

"No."

"Well when you do, spend time with them. Children are the most important thing in life. I realise that now. They are the one thing I think we should be selfish about. Our children need a sustainable world - not just a good one. They need to wake up and have somewhere to live. This is why I have been working on this new box design. If we can limit deforestation in packaging, we could add decades to the lifespan of our planet."

"I understand, sir. So you came home?"

"Yes. I sent a few e-mails and planned dinner, and then thought I would sit down and watch the game from the weekend before. I recorded it. I poured a drink and sat down at four fifty-two according to my clock. I wanted to make sure I'd be ready for Rachel coming home when she was done with her after-school activities. I'd forgotten she was going out that night. I don't remember when I last spoke to her about anything."

"Sir, please. Don't make this harder on yourself." In the process, please stick to the point, I thought.

"Yes, of course. I don't know exactly when I fell asleep, but I saw the clock said about five twenty. Then all of a sudden it was a quarter to six. Just like that."

"What did it feel like? Did you really feel like you had fallen asleep?" asked Norton.

Foxwood paused. "That would normally sound like a really strange question, but no actually, it didn't. You know when you fall asleep, you don't always feel yourself go, but you feel yourself waking up?"

Norton and I both nodded.

"Well, I did not feel that at all. In all honesty, it felt like I just blinked. I closed my eyes, opened them again a split-second later, and twenty-odd minutes had gone by. But that's silly, right? I was in a different place on the sofa. The recording had moved on. I must have just dreamed it somehow."

I froze at that description. It sounded very much like what had happened to me when Creeker had imprinted me with the false personality during my recruitment to the MSCE. I kept my face impassive, but I could feel the concern rising within me.

"Maybe." Norton smiled at Foxwood. "Sleep can be confusing some times. I had a dream once that I was on the run from the FBI. I woke up and spent five minutes planning my escape before I realised it wasn't real. I don't know where dream and reality crossed that time."

"Yeah, it was like that, but without the dream."

Norton nodded again and sat back, gesturing to me. I pulled myself together and thought where to go next with the questioning.

"What did you feel after you blinked?" I asked.

"Confusion mostly. You don't expect twenty minutes of your life to vanish like that. I don't like things that I can't explain, and this one has me stumped."

"What did you do?"

"I went into my office - it's at the front of the house - and worked for an hour, trying to shrug off the discomfort. I find it's the best way to stop something bothering me. It didn't work this time, so when I remembered Rachel was staying out, I called my friend Roger - Roger Sinclair - and we met up for a drink at The Frog And Nettle."

"We'll need Mr Sinclair's particulars at the end, sir. He may have noticed something that you yourself missed."

"Of course. Well, we went for a few in the end. I was pretty gone, to be completely honest. Then Rachel called." He broke off for a moment. "It sobered me up. I mean, obviously my alcohol level was still high, but the adrenaline overrode it. I ran home as fast as I could and I found everything as you saw it."

"Why did you wait so long to report it?"

"Because of Rachel. Sergeant, I got home to find my daughter in some kind of trance. I don't know what it is. It's like she just lost her mind. That dog was everything to her, which is bad enough, but to see something like that... It was terrible. And her voice. Her voice on the phone. I have never experienced anything like that in my life. It was her's, my daughter's - that was not in question. But it sounded like she was being dragged down to Hell."

25

"What do you make of it?" I asked. A police psychologist had arrived and was talking to Mr Foxwood. Norton, Harding and I sat in the observation room.

"I believe him," said Norton. "I'm sure the psychologist will be able to give you a professional opinion, but I cannot see how it would be possible to fake distress like that. I was actually feeling empathetic distress myself."

I knew what Norton meant. There had been a point when it had seemed like there was a lead weight in my stomach, pulling all my happiness down into the depths of melancholy.

"Which means we need to talk to this Roger Sinclair," said Harding. "I had a check run on his name. He's a welder at a local factory. He is not the kind of man you would expect someone like our Mr Foxwood to associate with."

"Earlier connections?"

"None. It seems that they met as a result of the beer thing that Foxwood runs. Means he probably knows Stoller too, but I can find no connection to the Wattler family."

"Then what are we missing? There must be something in front of us."

"Not necessarily," said Norton. "Not everyone is like Creeker or me. Not everyone has to be in contact with their subject, or in my case their after-image, if you will, in order to affect them. It's possible - even likely - that there is no evidence related to the actual murders that would give us any indication of who the criminal is. My question is: has anyone else seen the common link between these two?"

Harding and I shook our heads.

"They have both ruined lives. Mrs Wattler died, and her life ended right there. Mr Wattler lived a little longer, but was so cut up about what he had done-"

"You might want to rephrase that sentence, Norton," I said.

"Sorry. He was so distraught at his actions that he quite possibly committed suicide, but not before taking the time to apologise. The question there is who he was apologising to. Was it her, or himself, or us? We need to work that out somehow. I prefer that, in my mind, to the double murder scenario."

"Mr Foxwood's daughter finds her dog - her best friend - brutally butchered out on their back lawn. She is so scarred that she enters a state of whatever it is called medically. She is awake, but unresponsive. Foxwood himself has a significant conference coming up, but now has to deal with this blackout and his daughter, which is going to take his focus right off."

"Now we know that what likely happened is that Mr Foxwood committed this attack himself during the blackout. I would guess that the blackout is actually a period during which the killer's mind control of his victims takes effect. They would have absolutely no idea what they were doing, and they would wake up when the effect wore off with no knowledge of the act. Kind of like, I don't know, post-hypnotic hypnosis. Obviously Mr Wattler, for want of a better phrase, 'woke up' at the scene or found it quickly afterwards. He discovered his wife's body and presumably himself covered in blood, and assumed he had done the deed."

"So what about Foxwood?" I asked. "He has never mentioned blood, and he did not say that his clothes changed, either of which would have made him really question it all, rather than assume that he had fallen asleep."

"That's it." Norton banged his leg with his fist. "That's the missing element. It may not lead us far, but it's the one thing that we can see but cannot explain. Yet. How did he manage to embed an axe in a dog's skull, leaving that much blood, without getting covered himself?"

"That is a very good question," said Harding.

"How do we find out?" I asked.

"There is a veterinary forensics team examining everything. They should get in touch once they have completed their work."

"A what? We don't have one of those."

"They're out-of-county," explained Norton. "We can pull strings."

There was a knock at the door and Trisha Baxter, the psychologist, came in.

"I think I might have found something for you gentleman to investigate," she said. "I had a look through your report, of course, and he said something to me that I don't think you've heard." That would be the carefully doctored report that we gave her excluding the details limited to MSCE knowledge.

"Okay," said Harding.

"First let me say that I believe his story. He is genuinely distressed, and he is extremely concerned for his daughter. He has no recollection of anything during his blackout - or "blink", as he is choosing to call it - and he does not believe that anyone entered the property after that time or before he left for the pub. Therefore, I would surmise that the incident occurred mid-blink or while he was out drinking."

I nodded, even though we could have told her the same thing.

"However, he said that the nature of our conversation reminded him of something. He said that he visited a psychiatrist just before the incident."

"Yes, he told me that while I was with him."

"Did you ask him about it?"

I thought for a second. "Actually, no. Did he say why he was going?"

"No. He said he was not sure what had taken him there and, even stranger, he could not remember the psychiatrist's name or where he practiced."

"What? How could he have forgotten that?"

"To be honest, it reminded me of a case I took a while back where there was a witness who was a recovering amnesiac. Mr Foxwood bears all the same markers of that, except it seems only to do with the appointment. He also said that he felt compelled to tell a-" She checked her notes. "Mr Sinclair that he had been at work, even though he knew that he had not gone there that day."

Harding, Norton and I looked at one another, clearly all thinking the same thing. Who was this psychiatrist and could he be our killer?

26

Ten minutes later, we were in the car. It was time for me to report my work to Ashley for the first time, and we were heading back to the head office. I still could not tell exactly where we were going, but Harding had said that I would recognise the building when I saw it.

It was not a long drive, yet the silence seemed to drag out even longer than last time - but it was not so awkward. For my part, I was running through all the details of the case, and I suspected that the others were doing the same. I felt such a peculiar mixture of sensations. The individual steps of my interior analysis were so familiar to me in terms of detective work, interrogation and crime scene examination. However, the simple fact that I could not rely on any of the hard evidence in front of me was so alien as to be truly unnerving.

The idea of inherently unreliable evidence also gave me one horrible thought that I eventually had to voice out loud.

"Harding."

He grunted in response.

"How large is the MSCE?"

"You have seen all of us, at least in file form," he replied.

"Forty people?"

"Plus informants and Stranger associates. It is not common for a case to arise that requires us. There is usually only one going on at any point in time somewhere in the country. We can move around pretty freely. You will likely be promoted fairly soon, ostensibly to work for one of the agencies, and then you can work country-wide without question." He put air quotes around the word 'promoted'. "Naturally you will only be their agent on paper, not in practice."

"But is it not possible, even likely, that someone the justice system has imprisoned could be completely innocent?"

"I suppose so, yes. However, that would be an extremely rare circumstance. There is almost always something inexplicable about a case for us, and we get onto it pretty quickly. Our reach is long enough that we can prevent the obvious candidate going down for a crime committed by someone else."

"How?"

"Honestly? Any number of ways. We have a judge working for us up north. Evidence has been planted before to throw reasonable doubt onto a case, which makes a jury back off a conviction. We have even planted a jury - in totality for an exoneration or single members to throw off a unanimous vote."

"And how do we deal with the people we catch?"

"You'll find out in due course."

With that, Harding once again leant his head against the window and disappeared into his own thoughts. I shuddered though. That last question Harding had evaded enough for me to know I was not going to like the answer. The problem was, I felt that all of these concerns were beginning to cloud my judgement. Better still, doubt was blooming just as I was about to go and report to my supervisor, or whatever she was, for the first time.

We were after a man whose only discernible motive, at this point, was a desire to ruin people's lives. He had already targeted two people and could well be working on another, though obviously it was our greatest hope that such a suspicion would be proved false. However, he had succeeded in doing likely irreparable damage to one family and destroying another completely.

My question was simply this: if - and Harding admittedly seemed to think that this was a pretty big if - someone were to be put in prison for a crime committed by a subject of MSCE interest before the MSCE could get involved, was our very justice system, the core of everything that every member of the armed forces and the police forces and both foreign and homeland agencies was fighting for, ruining lives just as effectively as our enigmatic villain?

27

Back at the Penthouse, Ashley and I were down to business the moment the glass door of the meeting room slid shut behind us. She sat and listened to all I had to say. I went through everything that had happened in complete detail. She did not ask any questions or comment either with word or facial expression. As I finished with the revelation of the unknown psychiatrist as our primary suspect at this time, I felt that I had no idea what she thought about my work.

I stopped talking and she sat for a moment just looking at me. It took every bit of self-control I had to sit still and wait. She looked down and began to write, and my fingers began absently to drum out arhythmic patterns on my leg as I waited for her to finish.

I could feel my mind begin to wander as I waited. My gaze lingered long on the unsubtle hint of cleavage evident as she leaned slightly over the desk. Her ample breasts were pushed up by the surface, and I started to think of warmth and firm, yet soft skin. I felt the fabric of my trousers begin to tighten slightly, and gave silent thanks that the desks were not glass also. She was dangerous to me, I realised, as I started to peel layers of clothing from her in my head.

Finally she put her pen down and looked up. I dragged my thoughts from the gutter and tried to recover my composure.

"Good, Sergeant. You have done a good job. There are, however, a lot of questions that need answering."

I forced myself not to think of how alluring her accent was, and focussed on the question with all my will. "With respect, I am not exactly being given a lot to work with."

"That was not a criticism. I just mean that there is a lot of work still to go before we can sort this one out. Do you have any lead on who the psychiatrist might be?"

"Nothing yet, no."

"Are there any possible suspects that know both victims?"

"No. There was one, but he died recently. We cannot find another connection with both people."

"How narrow is your search?"

"Immediate contacts, business partners, school friends, societies. There's nothing we can find, but we're still looking."

"Good. Motive?"

"Nothing apparent. Both men were successful. However, Wattler died intestate, and has no family with whom he held recent contact. Next of kin is either his wife's family, or else distant family members of his own who are probably unaware of his situation. The Police report contact with her relatives, but not his."

"Foxwood has not indicated receiving any kind of blackmail material, so I am assuming no financial incentive, given both of those circumstances. I am wondering if this could be a serial killer - no motive required other than the thrill of the hunt. The dog as target could have been an unintentional aberration in his methodology"

"A perfectly valid possibility."

"Is there anything you can do to help? We have limited scope to continue the investigation until we can find the psychiatrist."

"Well, as far as I am concerned, you have proved yourself to the Executive. We are assigning you a new security status within the forces that will allow you much greater access to resources."

She flicked an identification card my way and I stopped it as it slid across the table.

"Home Office?" I asked.

"Yes. As a special representative of the Home Office, your presence will not be restricted by jurisdiction boundaries as it would as a police officer."

"Convenient."

"Besides that, there is little that we can do except continue working. You will discover quickly that a lot of our work is more frustrating than you are used to. You are starting to discover it already."

"I take your point."

"Can I ask about your experience?"

"You have to ask if you can ask?"

Ashley laughed. I realised that she actually had quite a pleasant laugh, and that surprised me. However attractive her voice, I had expected something colder.

"No," she said. "I just like to be respectful. I think that respect counts for an awful lot, don't you?"

"Absolutely. So ask."

"How are you finding Mr Harding?"

I was not sure what I had been expecting, but it was not that. I thought for a moment.

"He is a very thorough person who, I feel, needs to learn some social skills. He can be very abrasive to me, but even more so to people who are in vulnerable situations." I could feel myself tiptoeing around the question, but I was not sure whether this was another test or not.

"I see."

"Can I ask why you ask?"

Ashley smiled, but it was less friendly this time. Not harsh, but pointed.

"Because you are not the only one who is being evaluated. Mr Harding has been with us for a while now, but we evaluate all of our personnel frequently. He is also not originally a field officer."

"He was in MI-5, right?"

"Yes, but he was a computer analyst while he was there."

"Oh." That was interesting, and explained a lot. The fact that he had omitted to mention this detail also told me something about his character.

"Look, I have kept you enough. I am happy with your work, so go out there and keep it up. I hope to see you again soon."

There was something in those last words - a tone that I could not read - and I wondered at it for some time after that. I will admit that I dreamed about the possibilities a few times as well.

"One last thing," she said, as I went to leave. "What if the ones who were taken over were not the intended victims?"

28

Simon Jefferies opened the upper drawer of his desk. It somehow seemed fitting that in his study, surrounded by books and decorative art, there should be a pistol in the drawer. A short-barrelled, double-action six-shooter. Simon had always found the corollary amusing.

Moving like an automaton, he unlocked the drawer under the first and retrieved the ammunition box. He pulled out six bullets and loaded them one by one into the weapon's chambers. He spun the cylinder round and snapped it closed. Then he stood and waited.

At one point, he blinked, and for a moment he wondered what was going on. He looked around, confused. Then he blinked again, and resumed his silent vigil.

The library lived around him. A moth flew in through the open door. It fluttered around the room, stopping here and there. It sat on a wall for a couple of moments. It flickered around the window and in and out of the shelves of the bookcases. The flower on the windowsill slowly closed its petals. The sun peered in as it gradually sank in the sky outside, sliding along and up the walls, lengthening the shadows that moved around to hide from its gaze. It slowly blushed, filling the room with red.

All of this happened without Simon noticing. He stood focussed on the doorway. The light dimmed to a grey-blue, and on any other day he would have turned on the lights. Dusklight, he called this. When it was just that colour.

Finally a key sounded in a mortise lock. Simon's head tilted as he listened, recognising the front door. The locking bolt slid back into the door. The key was withdrawn and then another was inserted. The sprung latch opened followed by the door itself.

"Simon?" The voice rang throughout the house. Simon did not move or reply. "Simon?"

The door closed. Simon straightened his head and readied himself.

"Simon, are you home?"

Bags were dropped. The post was picked up, examined, and thrown back down. Footsteps. A tap was turned on, a glass filled and the tap turned off. A few seconds silence and then a glass put back down again, now empty. Muttering.

"Victor?" Simon called.

"Simon?"

"In the study."

Simon raised the pistol and aimed through the open study door. The study was located at one end of a corridor and the house entrance was down the stairs at the other. A simple, straight shot.

Footsteps. This time they were getting closer, coming up the stairs.

"Why didn't you answer the first time I called?" asked Victor.

"Didn't hear. Sorry."

Patience. Simon's finger grew moist on the trigger.

He blinked, and for another second he could not understand what he saw. He had never aimed his gun at anything. Was it loaded?

He blinked again and refocused his aim.

"What are you doing that meant you couldn't-"

Victor's voice was cut off by a surprisingly loud bang. Simon's arms jumped as he fired the pistol at Victor's appearing form. He recovered and looked down the corridor. Victor was nowhere to be seen.

"Simon? What the fuck was that?"

Simon did not reply. What had happened? There were two doors on either side of the corridor. All had been closed. Now the furthest one on the right side was open, and what little light was left outside was seeping through.

"Simon?"

"I missed."

"You missed? Why the hell were you shooting at me?"

Simon did not reply. A few moments silence.

"Simon?"

There was no movement in the house now. Then Victor's hand crept around the door frame, followed by his head. Idiot. Another bang rang out.

"Simon, seriously, what the fuck?"

Missed again. He obviously did not know how to shoot.

"Simon, I'm calling 9-9-9. I don't know what you are trying to do, but I am not risking anything else. Deal with it."

The sound of a phone being dragged from its cradle. Touchtone sounds - three of them, all at the same pitch. A pause.

"Police. I'm being shot at."

Simon ran the length of the corridor. He heard Victor scrambling across the floor. He dashed into the room and fired just as Victor's legs disappeared through the communicating door to the next room. He followed.

"Victor. Stop."

"You stop. Why are you shooting at me? Have you lost your mind? No, scrap that. Of course you have. Police?" This last was clearly into the phone.

Simon fired through the doorway to make Victor jump. Stop him talking into the phone. Stop him talking to the police. Not that it mattered, but it would get messy if they came. Simon did not like to be messy.

"God, Simon, what are you doing?"

Simon walked into the room. It was his daughter's room. The daughter that had died at the age of four in a house-fire at their country home. Unbidden tears filled Simon's eyes and he blinked.

"What?" he said, and stumbled back. "What just happened? I was in the study with a gun."

"Simon?"

"Victor? Is that you?"

"Of course it is, you fucking idiot. You were just shooting at me."

"I- What?"

"Shooting. At me. What is happening to you?"

"I... I don't know."

He blinked again. He raised the gun in the direction of Victor's voice and fired. His arm was starting to hurt from the recoil. It was not even a big gun.

"Simon?"

Simon blinked again. The gun was pointing at the edge of his Sarah's bed. He could hear Victor trembling on the other side, rattling her bedside table.

"Victor, I-" He put a hand to his head. "I don't know what's happening. I can't control myself. I'm afraid I'm going to kill you."

"What? Why?"

"I don't know." Simon was getting angry now. He was scared. Nothing was making sense. His world had been falling apart for a while now, but it was not meant to end with him killing Victor.

"I'm sorry, Victor. I have no choice. I don't know any other way."

Simon fired again.

29

Ashley's last comment bothered me. It had crossed my mind, of course. No detective worth his salt would utilise Occam's Razor as their only line of investigation. However, I had become caught up with everything that had happened in the last couple of days, and I could not say for certain that my eye was always on the ball in this case.

Had we really overlooked something so obvious and spent all our time looking at the wrong people? Were Wattler and Foxwood just weapons? Worse still, was my judgement being impaired by everything that I had discovered about this clandestine life that was going on under everyone's noses?

I went home that evening determined to get a good night's sleep. I felt as though I had not rested in a month, and I knew my limits. I was in need of rejuvenation. I would not get it in one night, but I could at least start the process.

I opened my door wearily, dropped my bag and collapsed onto my bed. I lay there, starfish-like, staring at the ceiling for some time. When I was younger, my room in my parents' house had possessed an artex ceiling. I used to gaze at the swirls and peaks that the material had sealed into when it had dried and try to discern patterns, repetitions or even words. I had found an upper-case letter 'A' once, and I used to wonder what that 'A' was the beginning of.

Now I had a flat, pattern-less ceiling, and I stared at it just to lose myself in the void of off-white. An ocean of blankness swam over my vision and allowed me to clear my head in a way that no form of meditation or music that I had tried could achieve.

I do not know how long I had been lying there when I became aware of knocking on my door. It slowly permeated the fog in my mind before it resolved into a nervous rapping.

"Coming." I pushed myself off the bed and back onto my feet. From when I had lain down to that moment, it seemed like another week of weariness had manifested, and my legs hung heavily from my body. I moved slowly to the door and opened it.

"There you are. Oliver, are you okay?"

The speaker was a woman, a few inches shorter than me, and informally dressed in obvious house-wear for someone I knew to be so fashion-conscious. Emily Randall would never allow herself to be seen outside in anything less than her best. It was not vanity - I knew that - it was a determination to succeed as a woman in a man's world. However many women added to the ranks of those in the country's elite - Prime Ministers, Committee Chairwomen or whatever - women attempting to climb the ranks of corporate businesses still owned by men faced a rough deal.

"Emily. Nice to see you too. I'm okay - just a little bushed from work."

"Oli, I know you. You know me. I will therefore be honest. You look like you just crawled head-first from a car crash. Minus the blood."

"You need to work on your flirting technique, Em. You're getting rusty."

"Come on, stop fooling. I heard from Harry that you have been coming back at all hours of the night these last few days - I even saw you twice, though you didn't notice - and Harry says that he hasn't seen you at the Last Glass recently, despite arranging it with you a couple of times."

Damn. I had forgotten again.

"I've just been busy with work, that's all. I have a pig of a case to handle, and I do not know how it is going to resolve."

"Then that is all the more reason for you to take it easy. Come down to my place. I cooked mac and cheese for myself this evening and made extra. You could do with a good meal and some company of an evening. Harry isn't here tonight, but he'll be happier if you would."

"I-" I stopped, looking at her. "I'm not going to win this, am I? Okay then. I'll come. Just let me change into something a little more suitable."

She smiled at me and walked away. She only lived three doors down on my floor - one of those crazy coincidences that life throws your way. We had been next-door neighbours when I was a kid. We had become friends after Harry and I did. I had wanted us to become more - I still did, I guess - but Emily had discouraged that with her trademark good humour. By chance, she had moved to my block of flats without even knowing I lived there.

I closed the door and changed into some nice-but-casual trousers and an open-necked blue shirt. I had no impression to make - I knew that - but it was not often that I enjoyed female company for anything other than business or more carnal pursuits, and so I thought a little effort would make the evening nicer still. I combed my hair and locked up my flat.

30

If there was one thing I could not contest, it was that Emily certainly knew how to make a good meal. 'Mac and cheese' was apparently her name for a cornucopia of flavour that happened to include cheese and pasta along with a glorious combination of herbs. Mine usually came out of a packet, and tasted like processed cardboard.

Emily had cooked for Harry and me on many an occasion, and it was one thing always guaranteed to make me feel better. We made small talk through the meal, sitting on her comfy chairs. It was a welcome moment of reality in what felt like a marathon of the obscure.

Once upon a time, I had looked at Emily the way I looked at other girls now. Then I had fallen in love with her, and I had seen her as someone I wanted to worship and be with forever. Now, both of those figures lived on only in my dreams. Despite my lingering emotions, her presence had become something calming, restful, and uplifting. I saw only one of my best friends.

We finished eating and I offered to help Emily clean up afterwards. She used the activity to raise what I guessed was her real reason for asking me to dinner.

"Harry is worried about you," she said.

"Why so?"

"He says that you haven't been the same the last couple of days. You've skipped out on pub trips without giving a reason, you look tired all the time, you're jumpy and you're working way too hard. He also said he worked all that out even though you are almost never at the station any more."

I chuckled. "You don't pull any punches, do you?"

"No. I'm a friend, and real friends are not there to sugar-coat things. I know we're not as close as all that but, since you won't speak to Harry at the moment, think of me as him for the night, and tell me what's going on."

I sat down, dish towel still in my hand.

"I wish I could, Em. I really do. I have been given a lot of responsibility with this murder case, but I can't talk about it. Not even to Harry."

"Why not? I know you're friends, but he's your boss too, you know."

"Not at the moment, he isn't. I am reporting directly to Detective Chief Superintendent Kwaku."

Emily raised her eyebrows. "That's a bit out of the norm, isn't it?"

"Yes. I'm not exactly sure why he's asked for it, but there it is."

Saying that, I realised for the first time that I genuinely did not know the reason. Of all the people assigned to the Wattler case, he had picked me based on previous work, but mine was no more exemplary than several of my colleagues. I wondered what Kwaku's motives really were in bringing me into the MSCE.

Emily thought for a moment. "Have you asked?"

"What?"

"Have you asked him? Why he is doing this?"

"Not exactly. He is not the kind of man that you want to cross, and he hasn't asked me to do anything crazy."

Okay, that one was not entirely true. To be fair, I was just continuing my police work in a manner of speaking, but the very nature of that work now had to come into question.

"You are a man with a badge. You have a chain of command. I appreciate that, I really do. I'm not asking you to question the chain of command or the command itself, but surely you want to know why you're doing something? Doubly so, when technically it alters that chain of command. Harry said something like that to me once when he was taken off a case. Doesn't the process mean something to you too?"

You have no idea, I wanted to say.

"Yes, it does, but it is just not as simple as that, I'm afraid."

She reached into my jacket pocket and pulled out my badge. She held it up, wallet closed.

"This is more than just a symbol for you, Oli, I know that. I was there when you got home the day your father died. I know what this all means to you, and I know that you got into this for your own reasons. Was it revenge you wanted? Or justice? Or a fair world? Whatever, you have moved beyond that now. You were a scared, angry boy the day your father died, and you were upset because no-one close to you could tell you anything, because he was away working a case. You're not that boy anymore. You have reasons beyond your history that keep you going. Make sure they don't get taken away, won't you?"

I wanted to hug Emily then. Just hold her close and never let her go. I do not know what I had expected to hear, but I got precisely what I needed. I didn't know whether I would go and ask Kwaku the next day precisely what was going on, but she had reminded me of who I was. I could not let events get in the way of my reasoning. That much, I owed myself and my father.

"Wait, what's this? Home Office?"

I started. Emily had opened my badge wallet and was staring at it wide-eyed. I had completely forgotten about the new identification.

"Oli, what's happening?"

"Em, listen. I honestly cannot talk about it. You should not have seen that, and you cannot tell Harry. Do you understand? You absolutely cannot. Not yet. I would be let go from the force if they even knew you had seen this."

"This is not just reporting to the DCS. What are you getting yourself into? Undercover work or something?"

"It's nothing, honestly. Well, it is, but not what it looks like." I realised that my fumbling around was not helping, but I had no idea what to say.

"Oli, look me in the eyes and tell me that everything is okay. Tell me that this is just something you need to sort out and that there is no need for Harry or me to worry. I need to hear it from you."

I looked at her. The deep green eyes stared back at me, and I wished I could just let it all out so that I could get the whole damn story off my back. I knew I could not.

"It's all okay," I said. "It's a temporary move, just while I work on this case. I've not been transferred or promoted or anything. I'm not doing anything that should cause you or Harry any worry, and I am not betraying him in any way. I'm just on secondment."

I don't know how convincing I was. I had not blinked while I spoke, and I had not broken eye contact. Emily gazed back at me, like she was trying to see through my eyes into my brain to work out whether I was lying or not.

"I trust you," she said. Her voice was convincing, but her own eyes belied a doubt. It was maybe not a big one, but it was enough. It hurt, because lying to Emily was hard enough, without being clumsy enough to let her see it.

"Emily, believe me, I cannot thank you enough for worrying about me. You and Harry always seem to have my back, and I feel like I have been able to do very little to actually repay the favour. You don't know what it means to me to have someone I can rely on. As soon as I can, I will tell you about this. I promise. It will make me feel better anyway, and hopefully stop you from being so concerned."

She smiled then, and I knew that I had won for now. I felt horrible for having done so.

"Good. I'm glad you are not angry with us for this."

"Angry? How can I be angry with my two best friends for caring about me? I am lucky to have you."

"You are, aren't you?" Her smile turned to amusement. "You know you have been wringing that towel out on my floor ever since you sat down. Do you want to tear it in two, or can I have it back?"

I flushed slightly. "Sorry," I said. "Give me some paper towel and I'll mop it up."

"I've got it, don't worry."

I stood up feeling a little awkward now that the tension was broken. Was I actually craving tension now? That couldn't be healthy.

"Can I get you a coffee?" Emily asked.

"I'd love it."

31

I slept well that night. I realised that I had neglected myself badly over the last few days. I had not been eating right, drinking enough or taking the time to give my mind a break from the onslaught that it had suffered. It is funny how little one appreciates the things that keep us going until they are no longer there.

I dreamed of many things. Emily featured a lot. Some of those dreams were very erotic, I won't lie. Others were fond memories of times now passed. One or two were a little bittersweet, as some of my childhood came back to me. I felt myself tossing and turning a little during the night, but never came any further awake than that semi-conscious state between waking and sleeping.

I woke up the next morning feeling, if not refreshed, stronger at least. I dropped to the floor and did fifty press-ups followed by fifty crunches - a daily habit I had not engaged in recently. Then I pulled on a warm tracksuit and went for a run.

Metal blasted through my headphones as I ran. I liked a variety of music, but always found the anger in metal music a good accompaniment to a run. It gave an extra kick to the adrenaline flow, maintained a faster beat for me to run to and I pushed myself harder. I funnelled anger out of myself and into my run, and came back dripping. I got into the shower and let the water strip sweat and anger and the last vestiges of sleep from my body and emerged focussed anew.

I looked at myself in the mirror. I still looked a little tired. One night was not enough to erase the bags under my eyes or the slight pull-down of my facial muscles that made my natural expression that little bit more dour. But I looked good. I was pleased with my physique. I was not in bodybuilder shape, but more what Harry called whipcord tough. He was being kind - I was not that strong. But I looked good.

I pulled on work clothes and ate a quick breakfast - porridge and black coffee. I had a little honey in the porridge this morning - I fancied something sweet. I glanced over the headlines, reconfirming to myself why I could not be bothered to read the papers. They were always so depressing.

Then I picked my phone up. I never took it out to run. Four missed calls. Damn. There was a voicemail left too. I listened to it. Harding was not amused, and wanted me to call him straight away. Not wanting to see him in any worse of a mood than usual, I did so.

"It's Soames," I said when he picked up. "Sorry, I was out running. Guess I didn't feel the phone vibrate. What's up?"

"Then put it on full volume, Soames. We need you to be on call at all times."

"Social call?" I knew it was not, and the insolence was probably inadvisable, but he was annoying me already.

"No. Another death."

32

I should have known that my moment of peace would not last long. Norton and Harding picked me up within fifteen minutes, and we were off again. Still, much of what Emily had said stuck with me. I felt happier about myself, and the mood boost was exactly what I had needed.

"So what's different about this one?" Norton asked Harding.

"Different?" I said.

"Yes. Harding said just before we got you that this case would not be the same."

"Simple," said Harding. "The man who was taken over fought back, it would seem. Pending your confirmation that it's the same Stranger, of course."

Norton tipped an imaginary hat to Harding.

"But you said someone died," I said.

"Yes. He did. He committed suicide instead of killing his brother. It took a while for us to pick up on it, but apparently the brother said that the victim had been confused about why he was doing what he was doing, and had had no history of mental instability."

"That's all it took?"

"We have an active search going at all times for things that sound related to recent or current cases," explained Norton. "It speeds things up a little."

"No offence, but your team are not always the quickest on the uptake," said Harding. I shot him a look.

"So what happened?" I asked.

"Difficult to say," replied Norton. "Maybe our mystery man got sloppy, or there was something different this time. Maybe his ability does not affect everyone equally. Without knowing its nature, it is impossible to say."

"We'll probably know more after I speak to the brother," said Harding. "The suicide could have said something revealing."

I balked. "Did you just refer to a human being as 'the suicide'?"

"Sorry."

Apparently that was all I was getting in response. I sighed. "Okay, so who are we dealing with?"

"Victor Jefferies," said Norton. "He's the older, and less successful, brother. He is an office manager for a data analysis company. Simon Jefferies, the victim, was the regional manager of a bank. The incident took place at his house. Apparently Victor visited regularly and they went out for dinner or drinks or what-have-you. By all accounts, Simon was not overly-enamoured with Victor, but humoured him."

"Who have we spoken to in order to find this out?"

"Victor's still in the house, and Ashley was there this morning. Called us on our way to get you. Local police are talking to neighbours and attempting to track down family. It seems that the parents are abroad. There's an uncle, but he hasn't responded to our calls yet. Police local to him have gone to find him."

"We need to find out everything Victor knows," said Harding. "This is crucial. It seems that the victims are genuinely unaware of their own actions, so we must find out from a first-hand source exactly what happened."

"While being sensitive to the man who just lost his brother." I could not keep the acid from my tone.

"Not if it impedes our investigation, Soames."

"Do you have a heart, Harding?" I saw Norton wince as I said it.

"Yes, as a matter of fact, I do. So do other people. If we push this guy, we might be able to stop someone else's from not beating any more."

Callous as he seemed, I took his point. Sometimes there was a need to push someone for the greater good, but I always struggled when it came to dealing with people who had lost family. Harry had led any such interrogations we undertook, with me playing back-up good cop. It looked like that would not be an option here.

Norton's phone beeped a second before Harding's and then mine.

"It's Ashley," said Norton, so quickly that I just left my phone in my pocket.

"What's she say?" I asked.

Norton looked up. "We've got a hit. Simon Jefferies and Terry Foxwood went to school together."

Finally, a connection.

33

Simon Jefferies' place was just as fancy as Foxwood's or the Wattlers'. It seemed that our killer liked them rich. There was the now-expected police cordon around the house, and I could see officers knocking on doors still. Two constables stood on either side of the front door. A crowd had probably gathered and dispersed - they always did - but a couple of small groups were still hanging around, talking to policeman or just watching.

We pulled up and attention shifted to us briefly. When three plain-clothes detectives, clearly none of them well-known, got out of the car, interest was lost again. I supposed that we were an expected development and not worth paying attention to. If only they knew.

I was impatient now. Not for the interrogation, which I hoped would be fruitful, but for a response from the team investigating connections between the victims. If Foxwood and Jefferies had a link, there was every reason to expect that the Wattlers might be connected with them as well.

Nevertheless, I forced myself to put all that out of my mind as we walked up the drive and identified ourselves to the officers guarding the house. One of them opened the door for us and, in a moment of total surrealism, I felt like I was walking into Number

Ten Downing Street. The house was stunning, and I could not help wondering what on earth a place like that would cost.

"Come upstairs first," said Harding. "We should see the scene straight away."

We walked up a grand, T-shaped staircase edged with ornately carved wooden bannisters. The walls were wood panelling and there were decorated windows and paintings at regular intervals.

"Hmm. Strange," said Norton.

"What is?" I asked.

"The paintings here are not particularly precious, which feels at odds with the rest of the house."

"Perhaps he has an affordable taste in art?"

"Maybe, but it does not match everything else. There are different design styles here that have been put together to create the aesthetic, and the paintings do not fit."

"You can tell that? Are you an interior decorator or something?"

Norton smiled. "No, I just have an eye for that sort of thing."

"I'll keep that in mind," I said.

Norton's expression became more sombre. "It's him again, that's for sure. I just got the scent."

Norton moved ahead of Harding, who had been leading us up. We followed him into a long corridor and up to an open door. Harding stopped by it, but I followed Norton as he moved on. We walked the length of the corridor, passing three other closed doors, until we reached a study at the end.

As with the rest of the house, it was smart and the decor had a foundation of wood panelling, but here it was a little more subdued, with darker colours and red furnishings. There was something serious about the way the room looked. This was a man who had made sure to have a place in his house to work - even I could see that.

"This is where it took hold," said Norton. "The scent is strongest here. Then he moved. It's fainter, and slightly different. It is almost as though it had 'gone off' by the time he acted."

"Is that possible?"

"I don't know. I guess it is. I know that people have abilities that have less and less hold over their target over time, but I have not come across something like this before."

"Maybe he really was fighting it. For some reason he could not be completely controlled, and so the power waxed and waned as he fought it for dominance."

"A good theory. I need more information in order to say how good, but for now I like it as an explanation."

"So where did he go?"

"Not far - just to this room here." Norton pointed at the first room back along the corridor, on the same side as the one with the open door. He tried the handle. It was locked.

"It doesn't matter," he said. "He went in there through the doorway Harding is at anyway."

We walked back down the hall to the room where Harding waited. He preceded us in. A chalk outline was drawn just inside a connecting door to the locked room. It circled a small pool of blood that had leaked over it from a much larger one just above where the outline's head was. Passing into the room - a child's, judging by the decor and toys - one could see immediately that the wall behind still had staining from where blood and brain matter had gradually slid down it. The ceiling was splattered too, though not so badly. The ceilings in this place were really high.

"The victim was here while the brother was over there," said Harding. He was checking against a written report, and pointing. "Simon Jefferies chased Victor in here, firing at him, and then asked what he was doing, sounding confused. He said something about there being no other way, and Victor put his head up just in time to see his brother shoot himself."

"Six bullets have been recovered in total. One from the hall out there, two in that room, and three in here including the one he shot himself with. Victor was not physically harmed other than bruises he sustained while scrambling out of the way."

"But he did watch his own brother commit suicide," I said. It was impossible to keep the slight note of contempt for Harding's unfeeling statement out of my voice. I saw his mouth curl in annoyance, but he did not say anything.

"The scene has already been stripped and reports logged. What happened here does not concern us any longer. We need to go and interview Victor Jefferies."

We walked back downstairs. On our way I could see into the corridor on the opposite side of the staircase. Another corridor stretched away from us, open and closed doors peppering its sides. This was not a house - it was a mansion.

At the bottom of the stairs we made a U-turn and followed a corridor behind them to the kitchen, a room much more modern and practical than the rest of the house. I stopped short in the doorway as I saw the scene before me. The man I presumed to be Victor Jefferies sat at a table with a uniformed constable standing behind him. Seated opposite him was Detective Inspector Harry Randall.

He looked up as I entered.

"Oliver, good to see you," he said, and then looked at Harding. "Who is this?"

34

I stalled immediately. Thinking back to my conversation with Harry's sister last night, I was not anxious to reveal certain facts to him now. Fortunately, Harding's almost cold efficiency preempted me.

"Detective Inspector Harding," he said. "I was part of a previous investigation for DCS Kwaku when this came up, so I joined Soames here."

"I see. You're the one I was told to wait for. Good to meet you, Harding," said Harry. "DI Harry Randall."

"Likewise. Soames has spoken of you."

I was pretty sure I hadn't, but I appreciated the gesture, nevertheless. Randall nodded to Norton. Naturally their paths had crossed before.

"Sir," said Norton, in reply. It was amusing to hear him address someone as 'sir'. The MSCE did not seem to pride itself as much on verbally acknowledging rank. I, for one, preferred that. It was not that I wanted to disrespect rank, or not to defer to it, but that the system felt antiquated to me. I always thought that people should be addressed in a way that made them feel comfortable and respected, and the few times I had been called 'sir' my skin had crawled.

Harry addressed Harding. "I have gone over the basics with Mr Jefferies here, but I waited for you to arrive before going into detail."

"The details, presumably, that are in the report we have? Nothing new?" Harding asked.

Harry stiffened a little. "Yes, the same. Nothing new so far."

"Good." Harding stepped forward and threw his jacket over the back of a chair. Harry caught my arm and leant in close to me.

"Where did you dig this guy up from?" he asked under his breath. "Come to that, why the hell did I get told to wait for you two?"

I appreciated the sentiment, and his understandable curiosity, but the circumstances were a little too harrowing for me to respond to his humour, even when it was driven by confusion. I smiled briefly, but made no reply. We sat next to a kitchen unit - Harding and I on one side, and Jefferies on the other. He nudged a tray in our direction. A decorated coffee pot sat on it, together with milk, cream, sugar and honey.

The service spoke of wealth. The aroma of the coffee spoke to me of quality. I was not enough of a conisseur to place it, but I knew it was the real thing, and probably not a cheap brand. The sugar tongs had more elaborate decoration than all of my china put together.

"Mr Jefferies, we understand that you have explained the chronology of events to Inspector Randall," said Harding. "We need to ask for specifics now."

"We appreciate that you have been through a horrible experience," I added. "But the sooner you can tell us what happened, the better."

"I understand," said Victor Jefferies. "Ask what you must."

He seemed like a walking anachronism. Looking at him superficially, it felt as though a bowler hat and tailcoat were missing. His brocade waistcoat in particular was stunning, and yet way over the top for everyday wear. At the same time, he sported hair little longer than a crew cut, and as he moved his head the edge of a tattoo became apparent under the collar of his shirt. His accent was East London.

"Why did you come to the house last night, Mr Jefferies?" I asked.

"Victor, please. Simon called and asked me to come. I was at a guild dinner in town when I was informed that Simon had telephoned for me. I asked the maître d' to let him know that I would call him back, but he returned and said that Simon was insisting. When I greeted him on the phone, he cut me off and said I had to come back to the house urgently and then hung up." He put air quotes around the word 'urgently'.

"That, in and of itself, was enough to worry me. Simon is not the sort to be discourteous." He paused. "Excuse me. Was not."

"Did he give you any indication of what was troubling him, or why you were needed?" asked Harding.

"No. I tried to call him back, but he did not pick up the phone. I was worried, naturally, and I left immediately. It took me about forty minutes to get home. When I entered the house, Simon did not answer when I called for him. I went looking around the house and eventually walked up to the West Corridor."

"Where the library is?"

"Yes. The second I stepped into the corridor, Simon shot at me. He didn't sound like himself when he spoke. He sounded... I don't know... flat. It was like he was angry with me, but we have not had any family trouble for a while, and Simon and I got on well."

"So he had no reason to hurt you?"

"None that I can think of. We're an honest family, rare as that seems to be these days. Our family's motto translates as 'Respect and brotherhood'. The two of us lived up to that. We care about our family."

"Is there any chance that he thought you were someone else?" I asked.

"No. He heard my voice and, besides the butler, I am the only one with a key."

Of course they had a butler. Honestly, I wondered how people like that could still exist in some degree of peace in this age of discontent with the upper classes.

"Where is he?"

"On holiday. I've been out of town for a while, and I only came back for the dinner. I was due to return to Germany this morning.

Simon suggested we take the chance to send Jameson away for a couple of weeks."

"What precisely did he say after he shot at you?" asked Harding.

"I asked what was happening and he just said 'I missed'. Then he chased me into Matilda's room."

Harding started to speak, but Harry cut him off. "Matilda was Simon's daughter. She died when she was four years old. Fire."

"What happened then?" I asked. I made a mental note to thank Harry later for annoying Harding, even though he presumably was not aware that he had done so.

"It was like walking into that room made him wake up from a dream or something. He was himself again and did not seem to remember following me. He said that he had just been in the study. He said that he was afraid he was going to kill me. Then he said that there was no other way and..." He stopped. "And he shot himself. I think he was afraid that he was really going to kill me."

"What was he like while he was talking?"

"It was like someone was flicking a switch. He was changing between sounding almost hypnotised and sounding like himself, but incredibly distressed. It would have been quite upsetting, if it weren't for the fear."

"Did he say anything about being forced to do anything?"

"Like he was literally hypnotised or something, you mean? No. Why?"

"Just a theory," I said. "There was another recent incident that happened under similar circumstances."

"What happened?"

"A man killed his dog," said Harding. "He claimed not to remember doing it, but the evidence is very strong, and there are no other suspects."

"How is that the same? I just lost my brother-"

"It's a complicated situation."

"It's possible that your brother may have known that victim," I said, before Harding could provoke Victor any more.

"How?"

"They were at secondary school at the same time."

"What was his name?"

"Terence Foxwood," said Harding.

Victor thought for a few moments. "I haven't heard the name exactly, but Simon did mention a Terry once or twice. He can't have been one of Simon's particular friends. You know how it was. There are the few people in the class you don't socialise with so much."

"Foxwood calls himself Terry. It could be the same person," I said. "I don't suppose your brother stayed in contact with any of his old school friends?"

"Funnily enough, he kept their numbers with his school yearbook. Those he kept in touch with, at least. Hang on."

Victor disappeared up the stairs, accompanied by Norton. Harry, Harding and I sat in the kitchen in silence. Harding's quiet was natural, but I had the feeling that Harry really wanted to ask questions and was waiting until he could get me alone. To fill the silence, I poured myself a coffee. Both Harry and Harding declined when I offered it to them. I had been right: it was a beautiful blend, deep and rich, and a slight sweetness in the aftertaste.

It was only a couple of minutes before the two men came back again. Victor sat back down and pushed the yearbook across the table to me. The three of us pulled our chairs closer and Norton leaned over our shoulders to look as well.

Harding opened the book and flipped through it. We all skim-read the names – somewhat unhelpfully categorised into five school houses and then alphabetical order – looking for someone familiar. Simon appeared on the second page. Numbers were written under a couple of people, but most were blank. On the fifth page, we found Terence Foxwood, but there was no number underneath his name. Harding sat back and let the book flip shut.

"Wait," said Norton, and threw his hand out to catch one of the pages as it closed. He opened the book again and pointed at a photograph with a number underneath it. The name read Christine Moran, but the face fitted a file photo I had looked at recently.

It was the face of a young Christine Wattler.

35

"How did we miss that?" I asked Harding when we were back in the car again.

"We who?" he replied.

I glared. "We the Metropolitan Police Service. All of its branches, clandestine or otherwise."

"Turn left," said Norton, interrupting the phone call he was on. "I'll explain in a moment." He went back to listening.

Harding frowned, and turned the car left onto a smaller road. "We were not looking in the right place," he said.

"Clearly, but saying that does not help us understand how the mistake happened."

"Do we need to? We missed it. Now we know."

"Yes, but what else could we have missed?"

Norton hung up his phone. "Actually, it was simple human error. Christine Wattler's previous name was listed as Christine Emerson. She was married once before, but we saw Emerson and assumed that it was her maiden name. No-one we spoke to after the Wattler murder mentioned a previous husband."

"What about her parents? Surely they were notified?" asked Harding.

"Yes, they were actually, but they have not spoken to her for years, and they were only tracked down this morning. It seems as though she was something of a black sheep to her family. They are not well off and do not inherit any of her not inconsiderable wealth. Christine also had the name Brent, which she took on when she ran away - officially changed it and everything."

"So they may not have known about husband number one?"

"Exactly. Rebellious daughter leaves home. Parents try to keep in touch, but she pushes them away. She gets married and it doesn't work out. She divorces and remarries. This time it works until she is killed."

"Have the officers responsible for the search been put under investigation?" asked Harding.

"For a simple mistake?" replied Norton.

"Simple, maybe, but do you not think that this information is rather important to the case? That maybe knowing it is going to reveal more clues?"

"Yes, I do. However, they were given instructions by you to focus on the husband, and so they flagged the wife for further investigation, but were not yet ready to follow up on her."

There was no malice in Norton's tone, but Harding flushed and shuffled his hands on the steering wheel in a manner suggestive of embarrassment. I thought about Ashley's comment that Harding was under review, but I said nothing. Besides, I sensed that Norton knew more about the story. "That's not everything, is it?" I said.

"No. Fifty percent of her estate has been left to Mr Ryan Emerson."

"Husband number one?"

"Exactly."

"So what happened?"

"Who's to say?" Norton shrugged. "There is one man who probably has a pretty good idea."

"Do we have an address?" asked Harding.

"Yes, and it's not far. Take the third right from here and then the second left."

"Who divorced whom?" I muttered.

"He divorced her," replied Norton. "He had to have a lawyer serve her papers because she would not grant his request."

"Does Emerson have a police record?"

"Not really. A couple of parking tickets and a warning for threatening behaviour under the influence of alcohol, but nothing more severe. The warning came shortly after the papers were signed, incidentally."

I took Norton's meaning. Emerson picked up the warning at the bottom of a psychological black hole. It was not typical behaviour, and he was likely not a violent man.

"Still, that's not to say that he might not have snapped. Did he know about the will?" I asked.

"Lawyer confirmed that he did. She said that she wouldn't change it even after the divorce - that he would 'remember her, whether he wanted to or not'. He said he didn't want it, and requested that she change it, but she refused."

"Well that's twisted."

"Yes, but it might provide a motive. Emerson was a key investor in Endrell Associates."

"Why do I know that name?"

"Accountancy firm. They're going under at the moment. Malpractice suit."

"That's right - they were in the paper a couple of days ago."

"Emerson stands to lose quite a bit of money apparently."

"How much is quite a bit?"

"He would be struggling on his mortgage in about eight to ten months if his business doesn't pick up."

"Then it sounds like we should talk to him."

"One last thing. Emerson's photograph is in the yearbook."

Harding took the next turn, his expression grim.

"How far down this road?" he asked.

36

Emerson's house was not a hovel, but it was not of the calibre of the others that had formed part of this case so far. Nevertheless, it was not difficult to see why financial trouble would cause him to worry about his mortgage. With house prices being what they were, no housing was cheap.

We knocked on the door and a short, weasely-looking man opened it.

"Yes?" he said.

"Soames, Home Office," I said, displaying my new badge. "This is Harding and Norton. Are you Ryan Emerson?"

"Yes."

"Can we come in?"

"Not until you tell me what this is about, no."

"It is to do with your ex-wife," said Harding.

"What? Did she send you? Or has she done something?"

"Why would she send us?" I asked.

"Because she seems hell-bent on ruining my life. You know she has not let me have a day's peace since I left her?"

"In what way?"

"Passively at first. After we divorced, she said she was going to leave money in her will to me. To remind me of my mistake, apparently. I fought it – I don't want her pity or her money – but there was nothing I could do. Then she sent a private detective around, and had him knock on the door. He said that she had sent him to make sure that I still lived at the same address, just in case. That was about a year ago, but the whole thing freaked me out. Since then, every time something bad happens, it reminds me of her. So why are you here, anyway?"

"Can we come in?" I asked again.

"No. Explain your business." I noticed that there was a weary note to his voice.

"Mr Emerson, your ex-wife is dead," said Harding. Way to go with the subtlety there. Still, Emerson had provoked that one.

"What?"

"She was murdered. We are here because we want to talk to you about her."

"Then you had better come in, because you're not doing that out here."

Emerson stood to one side and gestured for us to enter. We did, and were led through to a modest living room. As we walked, Norton caught both my arm and Harding's. We slowed for just long enough to hear him say: "Very likely not him".

Entering the living room, it was impossible to see anything but the television in one corner which I guessed to be about forty inches across. It was absolutely ridiculous to have such a thing in a living room with as little floor space as that one. It was also the only thing in the room that spoke of value. Everything was nice, and probably of pretty good quality, but it was also functional, not decorative.

"Do you want a drink?" Emerson asked.

"No, thank you," I replied. Harding shook his head.

Emerson walked over to a cabinet and pulled out a bottle of brandy and poured himself a double shot into a tumbler. He took a big sip of it and then sat down.

"Her influence, I'm afraid," he said, gesturing to the glass. "Every time I hear anything about her these days I need a drink. What happened?"

We stuck with the accepted 'public' story. If he were the killer, we could catch him off-guard, should he think we were fooled. If he was not, then we would have kept the security of the MSCE intact.

"It appears to have been a murder-suicide," said Harding. "The husband, Ben Wattler, seems to have killed his wife and then, in a fit of remorse, taken his own life."

"Seems to have?" Emerson was sharp, and interestingly lacking in emotion for someone who had just been told the circumstances of his former wife's death, however fraught he had been over her supposed harassment.

"Well, there were no witnesses," I explained. "It was in the middle of the day, and the only neighbour who heard anything was an old lady two doors down who heard yells. She chalked it up to abuse and did nothing besides worry. There was no note, as such - just a cursory apology."

I was not sure exactly how else to describe the bloody words on the wall without disclosing details we did not wish to share.

"Why did he do it?"

"We are still investigating that."

"So why are you here? Why are you questioning me?"

"Because the murder-suicide is not a finally confirmed verdict. It is... extremely unlikely, but possible, that it may have been a double-homicide."

"What?"

"There was an unexplained boot-print at the crime scene that did not match either of the victims. We do not expect to find anything forensic to confirm a double-homicide, but we still have to investigate the possibility."

Emerson's only reaction seemed to be a combination of curiosity and befuddlement. It was enough for me. If he were the killer, then he would have an A-list acting career for that alone. Murderers did not react the way he was. In some circumstances, it could be seen as too calm, but he just seemed perplexed by the whole thing. We could try to put him more on edge but, combined with Norton's subtle shake of the head to say that Emerson had no ability, I did not see the point.

"Does this mean that I'm a suspect, then?"

I changed tack. "No. In actual fact, we want to warn you."

"Warn me? About what? That I have a large inheritance coming my way that I really don't want?"

"Mr Emerson, we know that you are suffering as a result of the collapse of Endrell. This money could be a godsend."

"And that is what you have as a motive against me?"

I saw no point in trying to make my lie any more convoluted, and nodded.

"Yes, it is true that the money could save me, just now. The thing is the circumstance. It's not the murder. It's the fact that she saw this as a kind of punishment. The real truth is that she went on about it so much that she has actually convinced me of her malice as well, and now I see it as a very bittersweet gift."

"Seriously?" Harding's voice was laced with derision.

"I can kind of see the point, actually," I said. Harding raised an eyebrow at me, but I pushed on. "Truly. The circumstances are obviously different, but just after my father died a distant cousin sent me a rather valuable keepsake. This cousin thought she was helping. It hurt more than anything, and I would have destroyed it, but my mother kept it and gave it to me again years later. I treasure it now, but it was salt in the wound so soon after the event."

"Something like that, yes," said Emerson, smiling sadly. It was the most honest expression I had seen on his face so far. "But you said something about a warning."

"You were at school with your ex-wife, is that correct?" asked Norton.

"Yes, I was."

"Did you also know a Terence Foxwood or a Simon Jefferies?"

"I knew Simon, yes. Way back when. But I have not spoken to him since the last school reunion I went to. That must have been about eight years ago, I suppose. I heard Terry's name and our paths crossed once or twice at school, I think, but I wouldn't even call us acquaintances. What's this about?"

"Well, strange as it may seem, they have both suffered tragedies recently as well. Neither is quite the same, but it is possible that there is something organised going on."

"What happened?"

"We cannot go into details about the other cases, but it would be safer if you could leave town and stay with a relative for a while," I said.

"You think someone is trying to bump off my old school class? Do you realise how mental that sounds?" Emerson downed the rest of his drink.

"Yes, but it is one of our working theories. Most murder victims know their killer and, if it is someone from the school, then anyone who was associated with the three victims listed may be at risk of some kind of attack."

"I thought you said that a double-homicide was an unlikely event."

"We did," said Harding. "However, given the connection with the other two cases, it is difficult to fully ignore the possibility of an outside influence. Crimes are committed all the time, but three random, violent crimes with a root connection in such a short space of time would be quite a coincidence."

"Are you in contact with any of your other classmates, Mr Emerson?"

"One or two, yes, and I have numbers for a couple of others. A couple of them stopped keeping in contact after Christine and I split up. Why? Do you want me to call them?"

"No, thank you Mr Emerson. We would like to do that ourselves. We managed to get a few numbers from Mr Jefferies, but he did not keep details for that many people."

"Same old Simon. He could be an unsociable guy at times. There was no need for us to lose contact. He just stopped returning my calls. I heard that he got promoted at the bank to some kind of managerial role and I assumed he was busy with that, but contact never resumed. That said, I can't say I was that fussed."

"We have a copy of your yearbook here that Simon's brother gave us. Can you fill in any of the missing details?"

"Sure," said Emerson. "But, Victor? You got this from Victor?"

"Yes," said Norton. "You sound surprised."

"Well, far be it from me to say what their lives are like now, but eight years ago Victor hated Simon. He did not come to that reunion simply because Simon was there. If Simon got hurt and Victor was there, I would be looking at him."

Under any other circumstance, I'd have jumped at this suggestion and had Victor brought in for an interrogation. As it was, I had Norton's knowledge that Victor had no ability as a watertight alibi.

I just hoped that one of the classmates might be able to tell us something.

37

Emerson was true to his word, and supplied us with several contact numbers that we did not already have. Once we were back in the car again, and at Harding's suggestion, I called Harry and warned him that we had a possible serial killer on our hands and that he should contact the other class-members and caution them in as understated a way as possible.

"What is the M.O.?" he asked. "What should they look out for?"

"That's the problem," I replied. "We just don't know yet. For now, request that they take care if they are contacted by any old friends from school, particularly if they have not had contact with them for a long time. Ask that they call us if it happens. You know the drill - discreet, but urgent."

"On it," said Harry. "Oh, one other thing. You're going to tell me exactly what this is all about next time we have a moment." He hung up on me without saying goodbye.

I snapped the phone closed and looked up.

"How do you deal with persistent colleagues?" I asked. "No, make that persistent friends."

"Don't sound so worried," said Norton, grinning. "It's just a matter of deflection and intrigue, that's all."

"You need to dissociate yourself from it," said Harding. "It is best learned quickly. When you join the Secret Service, you do not even tell your family that you are applying. If you learn simple deception that early on, you negate one of the hardest learning curves."

"That may be, Inspector…" I put some degree of derision into my tone. It was not wise, but Harding had provoked me. "But not everyone is as detached as you are, and the rest of us have to face that learning curve. You chose to join MI-5. My indoctrination to the MSCE was hardly what one would call voluntary."

"You chose to join us," said Harding.

"Yes, that is true. However, I chose to join because I was given just enough information not to have a choice. If you were told that there was a monster in your closet, wouldn't you open it up to see what it looked like? You might not want to, but it is human nature to want answers."

"He has a point," said Norton, clearly enjoying the argument a little too much. He was in the passenger seat of the car, and I could see his eyes gleaming in the mirror.

"We are causal determinists, Harding," I went on. "When something happens, we attach a reason to it. It is a more scientific way of saying we are superstitious, I suppose."

"I know what causal determinacy is," Harding snapped.

"Then apply it. You happen to tie your tie a certain way one morning and break your streak of failed job interviews. Some with an open mind will associate the two. Now imagine if someone told you that you did not decide to tie it that way, but someone else implanted the thought into your mind. That is what you just told me, even if it hasn't happened directly to me yet."

"Creeker," said Norton.

"Good point." I nodded. "It has."

"Believe it or not, I do understand," said Harding. I thought he was a little unconvincing about it, but at least he was trying. "However, we do not have the luxury of time. You are not going through some training program, and you will not get a grade card when we catch this guy to tell you how you did, and a sweet if you get ninety percent or more. You will get a break until the next case, and then we go again."

"I do not say this to be unfeeling. I say this because you are now a member of the Metropolitan Special Circumstance Executive. That is a position of responsibility, risk, secrecy and little in the way of creature comforts. I am sorry, Soames, but the faster you recognise your position, the faster you can process and get on."

"He has a point too, I'm afraid," said Norton. His attitude was more serious now, and he turned around in his seat so that he was actually looking at me as he spoke. "I remember when I first joined the unit. It is scary. Nothing is what you expect, and you feel as though everything that you based your career on is up in the air. Correct?"

"That sounds about right."

"Don't worry. Everyone feels that way at first. Even this hard-nut lummox." He jabbed a thumb towards Harding, who growled back. "This is, what, day four of your time with us? It's a culture shock - just ride it out. You will have time to think it all through. That I promise you."

"You know, in some way that actually makes me feel better," I said. It did, too. I was not just being polite. "So what now? We know that Victor is not the killer, although he may not have been entirely truthful with us. We don't have any other suspects."

"Now, my dear Detective Sergeant, we do the kind of work that lives up to our titles. Deduction is our job, after all."

"Induction, Harding," I said.

"What?"

"It's a common misconception. Deductive reasoning would assume that we could take a pool of suspects and reduce them down to one definite. We have no suspects and therefore must increase our view until we can bring the net wide enough to include the suspect. It is not the desirable method, but we cannot apply logic to nothing."

"Smart arse," said Harding.

38

Thus began the drudgery. It was a familiar challenge, but with a whole new set of rules. We certainly were not in Kansas any more. Background checks on people usually told you a lot about them, but I was yet to find one that explained that the person was able to do something that the rest of the population could not.

Norton took the job of cross-referencing the names of the victims' old classmates against the MSCE database. He was one of very few people in the organisation who had access to that information on a no-questions-asked basis, and also probably one of very few who actually knew the identities of all of them - at least the recent ones.

Most of the time, I had learned, he was the one who finally confirmed that someone was a subject for the department's attention. I wondered if the MSCE had always been fortunate enough to have someone with his ability, or whether they had been guessing before. That idea worried me a little, and I put it out of my head to stop myself from becoming distracted.

Harding and I had the more unenviable task of going through the yearbook, cross-referencing individuals with the Criminal Records Database, and trying to find any history of action taken against colleagues, or anything that might have been referred to the police during their years at school.

Those who assume that public school children all grow up to be upstanding members of society are sadly deluded. They are well-educated - most of the time - but it is the person's choice how they put that particular knowledge to use. As the old adage has it, guns don't kill people - the people holding the guns kill people.

We found charges ranging from petty theft to fraud and, in one case, perjury. These were as colourful a bunch as any group of kids I had met. Looking at them today seemed to be yet more proof that we never fully outgrow our childhood.

Even though Norton was relatively sure it was a man, we could not take the chance that it might not be, so we searched everyone. Besides, we did not want to repeat the earlier mistake with Christine Wattler. An hour in, and Harding and I were really starting to flag. In an unexpected gesture, he sent me home.

"We're tired, and not working properly. Go home, get some rest, and be in early. We can pick up then."

I looked up at him. He was putting on his coat and putting things into his pockets. I wanted to leave, but I could not abandon this now - I felt possessed by some sort of fury.

"How can you do it?" I asked. I had meant it to come out angrily, but I did not have the energy.

"What?"

"Go home, knowing that this guy could kill again while we're asleep."

"First serial killer?"

I nodded. I had seen bodies before, but I had not dealt with this. The thought of someone losing their life at the hands of another human being was horrible enough, but for someone to be able to take multiple lives was a concept I just did not want to entertain. Yet here it was, served up on a plate.

"Fortunately serial killing is not a very British past-time."

Harding ignored my half-hearted attempt at mood-lightening. "You want to catch this guy, right?"

"Of course."

"Then you need to be doing your best work. Caffeine and adrenaline carry you so far, but not far enough. You do your best by being at your best. You do it by not drowning yourself in the case. Think of it as driving. You would not drive from here to Scotland and back without a break somewhere along the way, but you still get to Scotland and back in one piece. Without that break, what do you think would happen?"

"You're right, of course. I just feel like there is a bomb ticking and I am the only one who can press the switch to stop it, but I can't find the switch."

"To be frank, that is fairly accurate – though you're not alone in this – but even if we find the switch, we still have to press it. Given that we don't know who this guy is, we should probably be on top form when we do find out."

"Now there is some logic that I can actually use." I smiled, but it took effort. "I'll see you tomorrow, Harding."

He nodded to me as he walked out the door. I felt like a man in a scene from a film. Half of the lights were off and the pale walls looked grey-black, as if someone had spilt ink all over them. One bulb, in one of the meeting rooms, was flickering, almost daring me to walk up to the window so that something could jump up and shout 'boo'.

I packed up and pulled on my coat. Once out I considered taking an MSCE car and driving myself home, but I was too tired, so I flagged down a cab.

The cabbie began to make conversation but, once he realised that I was not in the mood, he fell into silence. I welcomed silence most days. Tonight, however, both it and talking were my enemies. Craving comfort, I considered knocking on Emily's door once I got home to see if she was in, but I would not be good company this evening. The Last Glass was definitely not an option.

The cab pulled up to my apartment block and I paid the driver. I needed something to take my mind off things, and so I called up my regular escort agency.

"No, Mr Harvey, I am afraid that we cannot send someone to you."

"Why not?"

"Because you frightened and abused the last girl we sent."

"I-" I wanted to defend myself, but what could I say that they would understand. I had thrown the poor, young thing across the room in anger and terror. There were not many things one could say to defend that.

"You may no longer use the services of our girls, Mr Harvey, and you may rest assured that we will not allow you to hire any other girls in the city either. You may count yourself lucky that we aren't involving the police."

By which they meant that I was going to be blacklisted by every agency. The phone clicked. I could not even find it within me to care at that point, and I let myself flop back on my bed.

39

I woke up the next morning at about five o'clock, screwed up into a little ball and still dressed in my clothes. I had not felt myself even beginning to fall asleep, but Harding was clearly right - I had needed it.

A great believer in the idea that your body knows when it has slept enough, I got up and undressed. I stood in the shower letting hot water beat down on me, and tried to imagine it washing away all the stress. It didn't work, but it gave me an excuse to stay in the shower a little longer. I screwed up my eyes in embarrassment at myself when I remembered what had happened the night before.

Thoughts are often rebels, I find, and mine wandered away from the embarrassment and on to Emily. These were not my normal, longing thoughts, but a way to release the other tension that still held me in its grip. I had never seen her naked, but I had fantasised about her many times. From time to time, she came into my mind, nude and unbidden.

I stroked myself in the shower, and wished the touch of my fingers could be that of her gentle mouth. I imagined her eyes gleaming, and her mouth wide as her body quivered underneath me. The hot water beating down on my back became the tips of her fingers drifting over my skin. Then my own body shook with pleasure as she smiled at me and walked back into the shadows of my mind, leaving the familiar sensation of guilt at defiling the image of the woman I loved so much.

Coffee and a bowl of porridge finished waking me up and I was ready to go. I caught a cab back into the MSCE office - we had to get dropped off two blocks away, for security - and headed in to get started.

The only other one who was in was the man who had played around with my laptop on the first day that I discovered the MSCE. I still did not know his name, and he was staring intently at his laptop screen with his fingers moving like lightning over the keyboard, so I left him to it.

I plunged myself into the work at hand with renewed fervour. It would be unfair to say that I was working like a demon, given that I was very carefully cross-checking facts and looking for anomalies, but it felt like it in its own way.

I had been at it for about half an hour when a female voice said: "Please tell me you did not stay here all night." I looked up to see Ashley standing on the other side of my desk. I had not heard her approach.

"No," I replied. "I got in half an hour ago. I couldn't sleep."

"Fair enough, I suppose." She smiled and wiped a hand across her brow.

I could not help but lose my train of thought when I looked at her. She obviously cycled into work and looked after herself. Her well-toned body was clad in a cycling outfit and she carried a helmet. She had a thin film of perspiration on her face, and my eyes instinctively followed the sheen of the liquid down much further than I thought was decent. The figure-hugging suit outlined and enhanced her figure and I just managed to stop my eyes resting on her large breasts. I crossed my legs with some attempt at nonchalance, hoping she would not notice the reaction that her appearance was having.

"You're in early yourself," I said.

"I always am. I am very much a morning person. Unless I have a good reason to be up late."

I was not quite sure what to say to that, but her tone of voice was more than a little suggestive. My fantasy from the shower came back to me, but this time it was Ashley walking towards me, and where Emily's gaze had been loving, Ashley's was positively wicked. I felt my throat go dry, and swallowed hard, forcing the image away.

"I get that," I replied, cautiously. "Once I wake up, I have to move - I cannot just lie there. More to the point, this case is bothering me. I want to prevent any more deaths from happening."

"Okay, I get the hint." She smiled again. "I need to go and get out of this thing anyway. Let's chat properly some time, hmm? All work and no play, and all that. And I like to play now and then."

For a moment, I envisioned her stripping out of the lycra outfit, skin glistening with sweat, but then I was brought back to reality by the sight of her walking away from me. She adopted a catwalk gait, crossing each foot in front of the other as she walked forward, hips tilted slightly back. My eyes did not leave her buttocks until she turned and disappeared around a corner.

What was her game? I did not like being unsure of where I stood with a colleague. I felt horrified that I was so openly leering over her. I had never felt myself so powerless to resist the wiles of a woman before.

The determination that followed forced my brain to focus solely on the case, and I buried myself in the paperwork, leaving my animalistic instincts to sulk while I concentrated on finding the key to saving the next victim.

I lost track of time, and almost did not notice when Norton put a cup of coffee on my desk and coughed to attract my attention.

"Oh. Sorry. Thanks," I said.

"That's okay. You look like you need it," he replied. "Incidentally, just for reference, you need to put in an appearance at the station now and then. People begin to ask questions if you're not seen for a while. You still have your police identification, yes?"

I nodded. They had returned it to me after issuing my MSCE ID.

"Good. To the rest of the world, you are still Detective Sergeant Soames, remember. You should probably pretend a little."

I grinned.

"There," he said. "That's better."

"I like it. A secret police officer hidden in the police force."

"There is a certain something to it. It's neat."

"True."

He looked over my shoulder. "Any progress?"

"Not really. I guess eliminating two more people counts."

"Definitely. How come?"

"One is already dead - natural causes - and one is in a coma."

He raised his eyebrows. "Yes, that would do it. Unlucky bunch, this class, aren't they?"

"Somewhat."

"You sure the dead one was kosher? No foul play?"

"He died of leukaemia a year after they left school."

"Fair enough. Then I'll let you get back to it. Incidentally, whoever our guy is, he's not in the MSCE records."

"I see. Is that good or not?" I asked.

Norton shook his head. "I don't know."

40

By midday, we had made no progress, but had also heard of no further cases. I fervently hoped that the killings were over, but obviously we still had to catch the bastard. Besides, just because we had had three cases in three days did not mean that the killer was working to any kind of time limit.

Harding and I both ate lunch in the office, sitting across from one another in complete silence. Ashley walked by at one point and made to start a conversation, but saw our expressions and walked away.

We were about to get back to it when Norton ran in waving a document file. He looked excited, and we both sat up straighter.

"What is it?" I asked.

"Something that we had no cause to see at first, but it may be a lead."

"Okay…"

"So as I said, none of the class is in the records - and there is no indication that anyone had cause to investigate him at any point. But, I expanded my search and discovered something else." He flipped through the yearbook on my desk. Harding was working from the back, and I had started at the front and, typically, Norton stopped in the middle, stabbing a headshot with his finger.

"Wesley Evans," I read. His picture was that of a very innocent-looking young man - the kind of man who would have been the butt of all the 'still-a-virgin' jokes at school. He had apparently aspired to be a chemist, and his "most proud" memory was winning a national science competition. The most embarrassing moment, which I doubt he had entered himself, was when he had been sick in biology when they had dissected frogs.

He had the curly hair – dull brown – and thick-rimmed glasses that were the stereotypes of a nerd, but contrary to the urban definition, he did not have the awful complexion and buck teeth of a science geek, and was actually not bad looking.

"Norton, he seems afraid of blood. This does not sound like someone who would kill - especially in the ways we have seen," said Harding.

"Maybe not, but look at this."

He thrust the MSCE file in our faces. It was for one Gordon Evans, who had been given the tag 'Subject 082669' on the file. I stopped at the number, my eyes wide.

"There are over eighty thousand files? I did not see a tenth of those." The details I had looked at were not full files, but briefing sheets with names and no numbers.

"No, the first two numbers are an indication of the subject's skill. Zero-eight as a start means that the subject has a skill that allows them unnatural manipulation of the environment in some way."

I looked back at the file. Subject 082669 was listed as only a mild risk, and seemed to be able to heat up liquid just by touching it. However, that was clearly not why Norton had showed me the file.

"I'm guessing he drank a lot of coffee," said Norton, as I turned the page. Harding and I glared at him, and he shrugged, an expression of good-natured resignation on his face. We looked at the briefing sheet. I vaguely remembered the photograph from the blur of images I had been shown when I started.

However, now it had more significance. The man was handsome, in his late thirties, and had facial hair groomed to be quite smart, if dated. He sported a pair of thick-lensed glasses that made his eyes appear too large and possessed a head of curly hair. The photograph was black and white but, at a guess, I would have sworn blind that the shade was a light, earthy brown.

"The father?" asked Harding.

"Exactly," replied Norton. "He did not show up in my search because he died before Wesley was born, so the file was closed, but Evans Senior is definitely the father of Evans Junior."

"This is genetic?" I asked. "Abilities, I mean."

"No, not that we know. This whole shebang seems to have nothing to do with evolution or genetics. It is simply there or not. However, there have been a few cases where there have been successive generations within a family, all of whom have some kind of ability. I believe the maximum recorded is five generations, but even then one was actually a cousin - it was not all in the same direct line."

"So Gordon Evans could do something. Going on the theory, even though it is uncommon, it is possible that Wesley Evans is capable of something himself."

"Precisely, though that would be true even if they weren't family."

"Will whatever Wesley can do be related to his father's ability?" Harding asked.

"No, not necessarily. Senior was not considered a risk at the time because of the nature of his power. He had a clean criminal record, with only a couple of parking tickets to mar that on the civil side. Wesley is obviously capable of something a lot more powerful, if it is him, but it may manifest entirely differently. The mind control idea is still an option, as well as any number of other possibilities. Hallucination, befuddlement - you name it."

"So we are at square two, perhaps - or maybe one point five," I said.

"Yes, but that is better than one, no?"

There was no denying that. Yes, it could be a whole load of nothing, but it might be something significant, and it was certainly worth following up.

"So shall we pay Mr Evans a visit?" I asked.

"Yes, let's." Harding stood up as he spoke and threw on his jacket. However well he hid his emotion, I could not help noticing that he was a lot more energised than he had been before he had gone home the night before.

Just as we were about to go, my phone rang. It was Harry. My face fell.

"Your enthusiastic partner?" asked Norton.

I nodded. "I'd better answer it though." I opened the phone.

"Oliver, where the blazes are you? It is not like you not to turn up to the office," said Harry's voice.

"I know, but I am out on the case again. Sorry, Harry. I should have called."

"You should, given that I am your superior."

"It's for The Quack. Again," I said, trying to sound exasperated. "I figured he would have told you." Norton grinned madly as I said this, while Harding frowned.

The change in Harry's voice was noticeable even on the phone. "Okay. I hope you finish this soon. It is not the natural order."

He was right there. I would have to address this somehow.

"Tell me about it. Look, I'll be back in soon, Harry. Maybe a couple of days. I have to go. Speak soon?"

"Okay, fine. Just one thing first – I called for a reason, though it really makes no sense to me. It feels like nothing, but-"

"Oh?" I interrupted him before he could go on to ask anything difficult.

"I just had a call from one of your girls. A... Samantha Jung. Apparently she had forgotten when I spoke to her originally, but she visited an old school friend about a week ago."

"Right. We'll speak to her, but what's so puzzling about that? We asked for any information relating to contact between the classmates."

"She could not remember who it was."

"What?"

"Absolutely no idea. She knew she had been, but she cannot remember who she saw, or what they were doing while they were together."

"Right. I'll call you back."

A sense of urgency kicked in. I hung up fast, and looked up at two confused faces.

"We need to visit Samantha Jung," I said, the concern audible in my voice. I explained what Harry had said.

"When did she call?" asked Harding.

"Just now, I think."

We looked at each other for a second and then ran to the garage.

41

I had never had such an intense car journey as the one we then embarked on. Samantha Jung lived some ninety minutes north of London. About an hour after we left, crossing the county border, we were joined by a police car, and I knew that more would be waiting at a discreet distance when we arrived at her house.

On the way, we looked at her file - not that there was much to it. Fortunately, the MSCE allowed us to access things like financial records and the like, which at least gave us an idea of who we were visiting.

She was the fourth victim of our killer who was successful and at least moderately rich, assuming that she was in fact a target. There was no comparison to Simon Jefferies - that was for sure, but she was certainly doing better than the average person, and had carved a successful career as a high-flying estate agent. She had a stay-at-home husband who, judging from their paperwork, seemed to live purely off her money. She was the youngest of three sisters, the other two of whom did not appear to have had the success or gained the significance that she had. In another situation, I would have suspected one of them.

It seemed that her parents had moved here from Malaysia - her father was a British citizen - when Samantha was just a baby, in the hopes of giving their girls a better start in the world. The parents' address was nothing extraordinary, which suggested that either Samantha had rejected them, or they refused her money. I suspected that they felt she deserved to keep what she had worked so hard for.

She had been very bright at school, but shown no particular wish to go into a more academic career, despite offers from several excellent universities, including Cambridge. A Professor Marks of Warwick University had even tried to head-hunt her at the start of her final year at school, following an excellent essay about the effects of cultural change on the economy of a country that she had entered into a national competition.

"If you were going to ruin this woman's life, how would you do it?" I asked. It was rhetorical, but Harding answered.

"Through the husband," he said.

"I'm not so sure. That is one way, yes, but look at when she got married."

There had been an unusual surge of anti-immigrant tension at the time, and one of the newspaper articles damning Marks' campaign on Jung's behalf had commented that she had married her husband at the age of eighteen, while still at school, and after less than six months of knowing him. That was unusual, although I would not have considered it suspicious. The phrasing of the article made it sound like they had committed a heinous crime.

"I know that journalists are not always to be trusted in this kind of situation, but if what is written here is true, she may not have much feeling for the husband. If her purpose is to succeed in her job, and that makes her happy, then he might be a glorified house-sitter. I am more inclined to suggest the parents if they are close, or the sisters if not."

"I agree," said Norton. "Something about her upbringing could have made her very self-focussed and determined to succeed on her own, not as a product of her parents' attempts to make things easier. She might want to justify the fact that she is here. She is probably quite sensitive."

"What are you? A psychiatrist now?" asked Harding.

"No, but I went to school with a boy from South America. He struggled to fit in and made a point of working particularly hard to earn the respect of his peers. We were friends, and we talked about it at length. You can be given better circumstances, but that does not make the environment that you find yourself in a positive one."

Harding made no comment. I assumed that this was his way of saying that he accepted the point. We drove on in silence again until we reached a staging area. A local car park, about five minutes' drive from Jung's house, was swarming with police cars. One group wore the SCO-19 designation of the Metropolitan Police Service's firearms unit. The others were looking a little confused by the presence of the weapon specialists.

"We're not in Greater London," I said, equally confused. SCO-19's jurisdiction was within the Greater London area.

"Benefits of the department," said Harding. "Shall we introduce ourselves?"

42

Harding's slightly taciturn and abrupt personality suddenly showed an advantage when we liaised with the other police officers. In no time at all he had them prepared for a three-stage entrance into Samantha Jung's property. We would enter as first responders to her call. The uniformed police constables would follow us in as guards, with more round the back watching the exits, just in case. SCO-19 would wait outside until such a time as we called, either to request their entry or to confirm that all was okay.

It was perhaps a little unorthodox, but so was the circumstance in which we found ourselves. I realised that I was getting worried that something would go wrong, and I wasn't even sure what that might be. Still, we had a chance here to save a victim and prevent a crime that we knew was going to occur. That chance does not arise often, and I was determined to get it right.

My train of thought was interrupted by Norton who caught both Harding and me by our arms and said, quietly: "I can sense him. He's not here, but his influence is. It's not strong at the moment, but it's there."

He stepped back as two policemen joined us while we prepared to enter. We nodded to them and walked up the path, with the two of them a few paces behind us, so as not to appear too intimidating to whoever opened the door. The house was the kind of thing I could actually hope to own one day, but only if I got lucky. It was a respectable and attractive two-floor detached building with a loft conversion and, judging by the old, partially-covered coal hatch to the side of the house, there was a cellar of sorts as well.

The door was not modern, but an old, wooden affair painted a deep royal blue. The knocker was simple, but very smart, and it had a satisfying resounding tone as we struck the door four times to announce ourselves.

Nothing happened for a moment, and I had drawn the handle back to knock again when a faint voice, distorted by tears and fear said: "Who is it?"

"Police, Mrs Jung. Can we come in?" said Harding.

"N-no. It's not a good time."

"Did you place a call to us, Mrs Jung?"

"Yes, b-but I made a mistake. I made a horrible mistake."

"Calling us was not the mistake, was it?" I asked.

"Y-yes. No. I… I don't know."

"Can we come in, Mrs Jung? Can we help?"

"I hope so," she said. The sound of sobbing continued, but over it we heard the door being unlatched. The hand or hands that were operating the mechanism were clearly shaking as we could make out the rattling of the metal knob on the inside.

"It's okay, Mrs Jung. We can help you."

I heard the lock click, and the door began to swing open, but only a few inches. There was a thud and following it the sound of someone scrabbling across the floor.

"Don't come in. Please. It's not safe. My husband is in the back garden. He can tell you. He tried to come in."

Harding nodded to one of the policemen who backed away quietly and got on the radio to alert the officers out back. I gently nudged the door with my foot and it swung in another inch or two.

"N-no. Don't."

The sound of footsteps this time - bare feet. Then a crash as something heavy collided with the door. It was not the weight of a body, but the door would have slammed shut, had my boot not stopped it. Harding held up a hand as he sensed the officers behind us move to protect us. There was a limited threat so far, and no evidence of firearms. It was a balance between entering calmly and risking ourselves, or entering hard and risking pushing her over the edge. We needed her to be able to tell us what had happened.

Harding looked at me and held up three fingers and mouthed the word 'gentle'. As he counted down silently, he dropped a finger per number. On three, I edged the door open again, but kept the resistance there. There was another bang, but I pushed back, and forced it open slowly. I found that there was no constant resistance back, but there was yet another impact - harder this time. As it gave way, I shoved the door and it opened.

Neither Harding nor I took a step, but a frying pan came flying at our heads, the hands holding it belonging to a woman that I just about recognised as Samantha Jung. Her hair was wild, and her face streaked with tears. Her eyes were wide and filled with the untamed anger of a beast, but there was an innocence in them as well that did not sit with the rest of her attitude.

We ducked back, and there was a colossal clang as the pan struck the door frame. I had to duck slightly as the next blow came inches away from my head. A third strike came our way, but Harding threw his hand out and caught Jung's arm. He twisted, efficiently but not too hard, and she dropped the pan.

Immediately her approach changed. She became close to a rabid animal and struck out with her feet and her free hand. Her long, manicured nails were a genuine danger to any eye they got near, and I had to fight to catch her flailing limbs in my own and assist Harding in restraining her. One of the policemen tossed me a pair of handcuffs and I managed to get them on while Harding held her.

She started howling and shouting unintelligible sounds. For a moment she seemed anguished. Immediately afterwards she was an avenging fury, and then just confused. The sound seemed to make my very core shake as though it were suffering from some great affront - both physical and mental.

We tried to talk to her, but she would not stop. She struggled against the cuffs, creating nasty-looking red marks on her hands.

She still kicked out, though we kept out of her reach. Finally, in an act of desperation, Harding struck out with a hand and hit her hard. Her head lolled to one side and she fell silent. Her feet kicked a couple of times, and then grew still. We managed to haul her further into the house and sit her in a chair. Harding appropriated a couple more sets of handcuffs and secured her legs to those of the chair.

While we worked, Norton came up to us and looked around, worried. "He's not here," he said. "We were right. Whatever this is, it's remote. She reeks of him, but he's not here."

"She's harmless for now," said Harding. "We need to talk to the husband."

"Let SCO-19 in - for show, if nothing else," said Norton. "And to keep them here for a moment. Just in case."

"Why?" I asked.

He looked down at Samantha Jung. "Because this is not over yet."

43

Supported by police constables, we scouted the rest of the house while SCO-19 officers guarded Samantha Jung and kept a discreet perimeter in the front and back gardens. As soon as we confirmed there was no-one else in the house, we thanked them and sent them home. There was no sense in frightening the neighbours by having a cadre of MP5-toting policemen on their doorsteps.

Another cover operation was put into practice, policemen standing by to explain that there had been a call from an over-enthusiastic (and unspecified) member of the public thinking that there was a hostage situation in progress. It was thin, but people had a tendency either to believe what the police told them or to know enough to back off, and we had been obvious enough that someone was likely to come and ask why guns were in their road.

The husband was indeed hiding in the back garden, and had been apprehended by the officers out there, but Norton confirmed to Harding and me that he was not the killer, and they released him for interrogation.

"Marcus Jung, we need to ask you a few questions," I said. "Would you come inside and sit down?"

"No. I don't want to go back in there."

"Don't worry. We have restrained your wife, and she is barely conscious. She will not be a threat to you."

"I don't care. I am not going into the house."

"Very well," I said, and we sat down at the garden table. Harding shivered in the cool air and frowned.

"Can you please tell us what happened, Mr Jung?"

"Very easily. I came home from a trip visiting my brother in the south of France. He has been unwell and had to go into hospital last week. I went down to keep him company and to help him with his recovery. I arrived back in England this morning and came straight home to surprise Sam with lunch. She likes a little Italian place we stopped at once on the way to the airport, and they do a good takeaway."

I became aware of the smell of food – perhaps lasagna. For a second, it smelled appetising, until I focussed back on where I was and why.

"So she did not know you were coming?" asked Harding.

"No. She had no idea. She was expecting me tonight, but I got myself moved to an earlier flight. Anyway, I came into the house and she was upstairs. I called up to her and she said something about not coming in. She sounded worried, which is not like her. Normally she will just say hello back and come down when she pleases. This time she asked me not to come in - said she was waiting for her mother - but I couldn't work out why she wanted me to wait, so I stood in the hall and tried to have a conversation. Next thing I know, she was charging down the staircase with a frying pan, crying and trying to hit me in the head. I got scared and hid in the garden."

"Why didn't you call the police?"

"As I ran through the house I dropped my phone. I was going to try and sneak back in, but she stayed in the window, watching. She did not see me hide, and I think she was just waiting for me to give myself away. I dared not move a muscle, so I stayed where I was, but it was terrifying. I have never seen her look like that. She seemed deranged, but while she was standing there she was pacing around and seemed to be arguing with someone."

"You said she was waiting for her mother?"

"Yes. That's what she said. But I spoke to Sepiah - my mother-in-law - this morning after I landed, just to catch up. She had not heard from Sam in a couple of days, and was not expecting to see her until next week."

Norton, Harding and I shared glances. I had a feeling that the same questions were going through their minds as were going through mine. Could this ability really make someone wait that long? Or maybe they were just deluded into expecting someone to come sooner. Did that mean the mother was the target, or was it all just a confused mess caused by the killer's ability?

"Sir, we have reason to believe that your wife visited an old school colleague in the past week or so. Do you know who it was?" I asked.

"What does that have to do with anything?" replied Jung, a little aggressively. I have often found that victims who are asked a question that they perceive as pointless get angry, though I have never understood why.

"Just bear with us. This is not the first time that one of your wife's school classmates has fallen victim of a rather unusual crime, and attempted to kill someone. We have to ask some irregular questions."

"Okay." He did not sound convinced. "I honestly don't know anything about that. I was out of touch while I was in France. We sent a couple of e-mails back and forth, but Sam got on with her business, and I was occupied with my brother."

"Do you know any of her school companions?"

"No, not really. There was a girl called Stacey she saw a couple of times a while back, but I got the feeling that they did not really get on."

That would be Stacey Monks. Her name was in the book, but we were not prioritising her just at this time because she did not have the level of income or the standard of living of the victims to date. It sounded callous, but we had to target our investigations carefully. The sooner we could pin someone down, the better.

"Anyone else?" asked Harding.

"No. I don't know her social circle well. We were not exactly what you would call... close."

"Do you know where she might keep her contacts?"

"Yes. She has a small box upstairs in our bedroom. She keeps a couple of bits of memorabilia in there, but also her address book. I'm not going in, but you won't find it hard to see. It's about this big..." He indicated the size of a shoe box. "And it is bright pink."

Norton got up and left the table and went back into the house.

"I'm afraid I'm a bit lost about all this. What is going to happen to Samantha?"

"Hopefully nothing," I said. I smiled, hoping to sound reassuring and hide the fact that I honestly had absolutely no idea what could happen to her. "We will keep an eye on her, but it is possible that this was brought on by a malicious event perpetrated by someone she knew at school."

Harding shot me a look. I gathered that I had stepped too far by saying that, but I wanted to get any answer that could help us track this guy down and put a stop to his activities. If it were to prove to be Evans, I would have him. If not, then I would find whoever it was and get them instead.

Marcus Jung nodded and looked at his feet. His shoulders had hunched down over the course of the conversation, and his spine gradually bent forwards like a tree curving under its own weight. He seemed to have recovered from the shock, and now the truth of it all was hitting him.

Norton came back out of the house carrying a book with a violently pink cover.

"She is waking up," he said.

"Please," said Jung, sounding desperate, "Tell me how she is." He straightened up in his chair a little more.

I nodded and walked in following Harding and Norton. Norton held up a page in the address book. At a quick glance, I saw that he had it open to the 'E' section, and there was an entry there for W.E.

44

Samantha Jung looked pale when we re-entered. She was breathing quickly, but seemed to have lost the anger and urgency that had been so dominant in her when we arrived. Where the woman who had welcomed us with a frying pan was a vicious beast, the one before us now was a shade-wisp. She almost looked like she wanted to give up her corporeal self and fade away into the gaps between the folds of reality.

"What have I done?" she asked, the moment the three of us entered. Harding nodded to the uniformed policemen and they left.

"I actually wanted to do it," she said. "I wanted to kill him. I mean, I didn't want to, but I really did."

"I understand," said Norton. "But it was not really you that wanted your husband killed, was it?"

"No. I don't think it was. I certainly wasn't myself. Am I going mad? Am I losing my mind?"

"No, Samantha, you are not."

"But it's worse. I felt like I wanted him dead for being in the way. I felt like it wasn't him I really wanted to kill."

"Who did you want to kill?" I asked.

"I don't know. I just know that it wasn't really him, but he wouldn't go away."

"It was not you," said Norton, emphatically. "It really was not. We believe that you may have been under someone else's influence."

"What? How?"

"We don't know yet," said Harding. "We were hoping you could tell us."

"But I don't know about things like that. Can people even do that?"

"You called the police earlier about visiting a friend."

"Did I?"

"You did," said Norton. "You were phoned by a policeman called Detective Inspector Harry Randall, and he said to call him if you had any unexpected contact with people you had known at school. You rang back earlier to say that you had visited someone a week ago, but could not remember who or why."

"Oh yes," she said, and her voice sounded distant and ghostly. "I did, didn't I?"

"Do you know who it was, Samantha?"

"Who what was? Oh. I… I don't remember."

"Please try," I said. "It is really important that you tell us anything and everything that you can. Several people's lives have been ruined already, including yours, and we might be able to stop someone else from suffering the same way."

She struggled to think. It is a common saying that you can almost see the cogs in someone's mind working, but we really could. Her eyebrows furrowed and raised and flicked in all different directions as she obviously really had to try in order to think.

"I remember. It was last week, wasn't it?" she said, finally.

"Yes, it was. Do you remember who you went to see?" asked Norton.

"Yes. Someone short. Much shorter than me. I don't remember exactly. I know it was someone… Oh…" She grasped her head with her hands.

"Don't worry. Take a few moments to get your head together. You have just been through a terrible experience."

Hurry up, I was thinking. We are so close I can almost smell this guy, but we are just not close enough. I was itching for her just to say a name so that we could go and get the bastard. I would not rest until he was locked away.

Suddenly I realised how Harding must deal with things, and I knew that I did not want to become like him. It is always important to care what happens, and you should never just decide someone's fate in advance of an opportunity to understand every angle of the story.

I just wondered what chance we had of ever getting the full story...

"It was Wesley," she said. "It was Wesley Evans that I went to see."

We had the name – confirmation, at last.

45

Typically, Evans lived on the other side of London, and by now the evening rush hour was in full force. Of course, we had the advantage of being in a police vehicle. Although it was an MSCE one, it still had interior 'blues and twos' - the police lights and siren. Harding turned them on, and we shot off, leaving the police constables at the Jung's house making arrangements for Samantha to be taken into protective custody for her own safety.

There is nothing quite so exhilarating as driving through London at breakneck speed. Given how difficult a city it can be to get through as a civilian - and how unreliable the roads that circumnavigate it are - there is always a sense of somehow cheating the system.

This time, however, we were singularly focussed on getting Evans. Curses were yelled out by all three of us as people did not get out of our way quickly enough or we came across road-works or traffic jams that held us up. Where previously the tension in the car had been due to awkwardness, now it was a palpable sense of nervousness and excitement as we neared the finale to a traumatic few days.

None of us spoke to any of the others. We just watched as the city flashed by. Harding was concentrating on driving, Norton was trying to read up on Wesley's file, and I was sitting in the back drumming my heels into the floor of the car and my hands into my knees.

We left London finally and hit wider roads, where overtaking and fast driving were easier. We were, by now, in convoy with two SCO-19 vehicles as well as two Metropolitan Police vehicles. A black car with tinted windows had pulled up next to us also, and Harding had nodded in its direction, so I presumed the occupants to be MI-5. Two other tinted four-by-fours were also with us containing members of the MSCE. Apparently the denouement of a case in this department was quite a social occasion.

Passing through Sevenoaks, we were joined by the local force, and we continued on for some minutes driving through ever-narrowing back streets and country lanes until we were prepared to set up a staging area half a mile from Evans' home - an out-of-the-way farm called Marshall's Watch.

The local police drew up and Norton moved away to brief them. Their role was mostly to form a perimeter and stop the escape of anyone from within, while also keeping people at bay. Until we understood the true nature of Evans' skill, we did not want to offer him anything in the way of human bargaining chips. It was a gamble we would be almost sure to lose.

SCO-19 were briefed by Ashley who had arrived in one of the MSCE vehicles with DCS Kwaku. They were told a little more - that Evans was implicated in the deaths of at least three individuals and the attempted murder of one more, that he was to be considered highly dangerous even if unarmed, and that they were only to shoot as an absolute last resort.

Kwaku came over to me and Harding. He exchanged a few words with Harding before the latter left to speak to the MI-5 agents.

"It will be interesting to see what they make of this," said Kwaku. He watched the two men the agency had sent very carefully. Without taking his eyes off them, he continued. "MI-5 knows of our existence, of course. There would be no way of keeping it secret from them. It also allows us at least a little inter-agency cooperation, rather than leaving us out on our own."

"However, they do not know the full extent of what it is we do or deal with. They will not approach you, so it will not be a problem, but I will ask that you do not say anything to them about us. The only exact details they know are the names of the agents. We have to do some pretty unorthodox things at times, and it saves complications. They are only here to observe. All of our operations are monitored by SIS. They are suspicious of us, and rightly so, I suppose."

Finally Kwaku looked away from the men. He seemed satisfied by what he had observed, though I had only seen Harding and the two others talking, with no indication of emotion or reaction on any front. Then again, that might have been the exact thing that Kwaku was looking for.

"I am sorry, Detective Sergeant Soames."

I blinked in surprise at the statement and looked at Kwaku. He was looking directly at me and, for the first time, I detected a true sense of caring in his expression. Here was a man who took a lot of stick from his men, and yet he still felt for them, even if he only chose to show it occasionally. I found, in that moment, that my respect for the Detective Chief Superintendent went up immensely.

"For what, sir?" I asked.

"For throwing you quite so bodily into the deep end. Naturally I did not know the course this case would take, and while most of those cases that we take on are less than savoury, this has been particularly unpleasant. You have seen some horrible things, and had to deal with an awful lot in a very short space of time."

"That's okay, sir," I said, with a levity that I thought was not entirely forced. "I enjoy a challenge."

Kwaku smiled. "I know. It's one of the reasons I picked you for the department. Just take a little time after you finish this to rest and relax. Wind-down time is very important."

I wondered why he was bringing all of this up now. I also wanted to ask him what the other reasons for my recruitment were, but I knew that this was not the time.

"There is a conference I want you to attend once this is done. I think that you will find it very beneficial, and I hope the scenery will be to your taste."

"Oh? Where is it, sir?"

"In a cocktail bar on the Costa Del Sol."

Kwaku laughed quietly. I had never heard him laugh before, but in his rich basso, it was a jovial sound and I found myself caught up in the moment and chuckling. I realised that it was the most honest smile I had worn for days. I had no idea whether he was joking about me taking time off, but he had lightened my mood, and I suspected that therein lay the result he had been seeking.

A moment later, his expression became more serious.

"Take care of yourself in there, Soames. You have made a promising start in this department, and I would like to see you work for us more in the future. We may not know what this man Evans can do, but be ready for anything."

"Yes, sir. I will be."

"Good. Now then. Let's go and hurry the troops along a little, shall we?"

46

The plans were laid, and the pieces were in place. All that remained was to start the game, stick to the strategy, and hope that we won. In what was a three-stage deployment process, the police began by setting up the perimeter. A quarter of a mile in every direction was sealed off. There were only half a dozen roads in the area, but policemen were sent to country paths, cycle routes and other methods of access to make sure that no innocents got caught up in whatever might happen.

There were some twenty-odd houses in the area as well, spread out among the farmland and fields, and officers went to each of them asking the residents to remain in their homes where possible.

In the next stage, SCO-19 approached the house. They engaged in rapid long-range surveillance to begin with. Detecting no movement, they placed a couple of snipers in position to watch the house, armed with Heckler and Koch G3k assault rifles. Then officers toting MP5s and Glock 17s rushed the boundaries of the house, and infiltrated up to the walls, windows and doors. Cameras and microphones were deployed, and feedback given that there was no indication of anyone moving inside.

In an ideal world, we would have had a helicopter up to conduct a thermal scan on the area, but for some reason it had not arrived. The perimeter was as secure as we could make it, but

I couldn't help feeling that the extra cover would have eased the pressure a little.

Finally, the Metropolitan Special Circumstance Executive moved in. Harding and I simply walked through the front gate and up the path, in full view and with no stealth whatsoever. Creeker came with us, poised to grab Evans in an attempt to exert his ability's influence over him. When we reached the door, Harding banged on it and, with a practiced air shouted: "Police. Open the door."

SCO-19 officers flanked us on both sides, sidearms ready to be brought to bear on whoever opened the door. Nothing happened. Harding called out again.

"Wesley Evans, this is the police. Open the door now or we will be forced to break it down."

When there was still no response, Harding stepped back and nodded to the two SCO-19 men. The two men looked at each other and one counted to three silently. On three, they kicked the door down and charged the house. Seconds later, I heard other officers breach the back door as well, while others knocked in the windows.

We followed them in immediately and scouted the house. It was quick and efficient. Norton and Ashley followed the men who came in the back and searched downstairs. Harding and I went up with the two who had breached the front door. There was no-one there.

Harding cried out wordlessly in frustration. Radio silence was broken, and we heard communications flashing between officers. There was no-one in sight. Evans was not here, and we had no idea where he might be. Was he out trying to attack someone else? Had he known we were coming somehow? Was he just getting groceries and might return at a moment's notice? The nearest shops were some way away. Plain-clothes men were already en route to make a covert sweep for him, and the SCO-19 officers began to withdraw and prepare for re-deployment wherever was necessary.

Harding stood watching the withdrawal, waiting to speak to MI-5, I supposed. Norton, Ashley and I began to search the house for clues.

The first thing that struck me was that the house was not extravagant. Property records showed that, although the house was called Marshall's Watch Farm, most of the land around had been purchased by adjacent landholders - either farmers or just people who lived nearby and wanted to expand their land. The estate of Marshall's Watch had declined substantially over the last hundred years.

It took us very little time to search. Evans had either lost money or never had it, and he possessed very little. He had a great interest in chemistry, as was evidenced by books and scientific periodicals dotted around. He had no art, and just a couple of photographs up on the walls, most likely taken by local semi-professional photographers. Furniture was spartan, and there was nowhere in the place for him to hide. Neither were there any clues to his location.

Our frustration grew as we continued to search and reports came back from other officers that he was nowhere to be seen within a five mile area. Neighbours confirmed that he was rarely away from the farm, but that they had occasionally seen other cars parked in his driveway when passing by. Fortunately the farm buildings fronted onto the road, and so much was visible. However, none had taken registration plates for any reason, and so we could not confirm that our victims were recent visitors.

"We got ahead of ourselves," said Harding, after another negative report came in.

"No. He just gave us the slip, intentionally or otherwise," said Kwaku. I had not heard him enter the house. "We have the advantage, as of this moment, in every way except his skill. He may not even know that we are onto him."

"Then what do we do next?"

"Hang on," I said. "I've just thought of something."

All four of the other MSCE members turned to look at me.

"If he is such a chemistry buff, why does he not have any evidence of it other than books and papers? Where is his apparatus? Surely every chemist without a lab would play around a little at home, but if you disregard the literary material, there is no evidence here that he is involved in science at all."

"So you are thinking that he might be something else?" asked Ashley.

"No. Somewhere else," I replied. "What if he has a lab - official or otherwise, and I'm guessing the latter - that we don't know about?"

47

Every now and then, you come across a situation that takes forever to resolve. You find yourself having to go through endless financial or property records to try to chase down a trail. You have to interrogate people who do not actually know what you need to know at the time. For whatever reason, your investigation suddenly takes a turn for the snail-paced.

By some extraordinary coincidence, this turned out not to be one of those times. A police constable, assigned to a wooded path a quarter of a mile away, suddenly came on the radio reporting the discovery of a prefabricated building that was not listed on any of the maps that we had been provided with. It was not large, but it definitely had power, as there was light shining from a window, even though it was not yet dark.

He could not get close enough to register movement without giving himself away, but we did not care. Right at that moment, that building was our best opportunity to end this quickly and safely.

Even so, there should have been protocols to follow but, perhaps by way of establishing a balance of karma after finding the structure so easily, they were stopped when the police officer who found it came back on the radio.

"Sir, I just heard a scream from inside," he said.

Norton's face blanched, and even Kwaku looked a little unsettled.

"He's got someone in there," said Harding. "We need to go."

I was pleasantly surprised to hear the urgency in his voice.

"We have no chemical protection," said Norton. "We cannot go in without knowing what we are facing. Who knows what he is cooking up in there? Given how variable his control has been, if he is using some kind of hallucinogen or hypnosis-inducing drug, we have no idea what it contains. Obviously it is adjusted by him, or else no trace of his ability would show, but I cannot say what form that adjustment takes."

"Sir, what should I do? Something bad is going on." The crackling on the radio did not hide the officer's discomfort, and we heard the beginning of a shriek as he let go of the transmit button.

"Goddammit, we have to go," I said, and took off for the coordinates the officer had given. I heard pounding feet, and realised that Harding was beside me. I was being reckless, I knew that, but I did not know what else to do. I heard orders being shouted as we ran, and glanced back to see the other officers beginning to converge behind us, moving en masse in the same direction we were.

As we got closer we slowed down, and got our first glimpse of the building. It was hardly the most prepossessing of structures - a dull, off-military-green prefab that looked cheap. The roof was cracked in one corner and the windows, though they had full sheets of glass in them, were covered with torn mosquito netting.

The door seemed to loom up before us. Chipped red paint covered it like a massive warning sign, and it seemed to have a power over us for a second. Then the silence broke and chatter began again. I could hear Kwaku ordering us to wait, probably on our private channel.

I could not do that, though. From up ahead of us came the sound of chirping, and the rustle of the wind through the trees, and from behind, I could hear other birds taking wing as men disturbed them. However, piercing through nature's chorus, I could just make out the sound of sobbing from inside the structure. My blood was up now, and I was not about to let this madman ruin any more lives, or to hurt whatever poor woman he had in there any more than he had already.

The perimeter of the structure could have been no more than fifty paces, and it only had the one door. Harding and I approached swiftly, flanked by SCO-19 officers who had donned gas masks.

"We're with you, sir," one said.

They passed a gas mask to each of us, and we pulled them over our heads, muttering our thanks. One of the armed men moved to the door and put his hand to the handle, while the other readied his weapon. Harding nodded, and the first officer tried the handle, very gently. It turned, and the door opened. Clearly our target was not expecting visitors.

With a bang, the officer threw the door open, and the two men entered, sweeping their weapons around to cover all areas of the room. There was a stifled shriek from the woman. Harding leaned around the doorframe and called out: "Armed police. Wesley Evans, come out with your hands above your head." His voice was distorted by the mask, but clearly audible. There was no reply.

Even as Harding and I moved in, SCO-19 were already breaching the two doors we discovered inside the structure. It was indeed a laboratory of sorts. Various chemical apparatus dotted the room on benches. Some I recognised from my days at school, such as retorts and bunsen burners. Others were familiar only by shape, and one or two appeared to have been custom made.

Coloured chemicals sat in the bowls of the various glass pieces and, following the apparent daisy-chain of the experiment, I spotted a few bottles containing an almost-clear liquid – presumably the result of the process. It looked like something out of a child's television show, but it had a much more insidious feeling given the circumstances.

Nothing seemed to be bubbling, or looked likely to explode. Still, we did not want to break any one of those vials. I made sure that the door stayed open to let out any gas that was present in the room.

Having established the low chance of any danger, as best I could, I turned to the woman. She was strapped to a chair facing the door we had entered by, and sobbing silently, tears streaking down her cheeks. I recognised her from the yearbook, but could not put a name to the face.

"Where is he?" I asked, softly. She frowned at me, and I realised that the gas mask was distorting my voice, just as Harding's had done. I asked again, slightly louder this time, and she shook her head and shrugged.

Three shouts of 'Clear' rang through the building. I cursed and my heart fell. After all that, Wesley Evans was not here. I turned back to the door and saw a similar deflation in Ashley and Norton, now standing in the doorway, also wearing masks. Even Harding's impassive face dropped a little.

I moved and spoke to the woman, untying her bonds as I did.

"You're safe now," I said, although I did not believe that. "What is your name? What did he do to you?"

She looked back at me with wide eyes and continued to cry. Even though her hands and legs were free, she gripped the arms of the chair hard, and did not move. The gas mask was probably frightening her, but I did not want to take it off. I tried talking as comfortingly as I could, but gave it up before I made things worse.

One of the SCO-19 men turned to us holding a device I did not recognise and pulled off his mask.

"We're safe," he said. "Nothing in the air that I can detect."

I was tempted to wait a second, to see if he still thought that after he had taken a few breaths of the air, but Harding, Ashley, and Norton pulled their masks off immediately, so I followed suit. I turned back to the woman again.

"I'm sorry," I said. I spoke slowly, and put as much feeling as I could into my voice. "I did not mean to scare you. What did he do to you?"

Her voice was halting, and she stopped several times to cry more, but I gathered that she had come to visit Evans because he had sent an e-mail stating that he had heard she was in trouble with her finances, and he could help her. He was a psychiatrist, he said, and he wanted to help old friends. She thought it was odd, but she did not know where else to turn.

When she got to the house, he said that he had a cabin a short way into the woods, and that it was the perfect place for privacy. She had declined to follow him, but he had produced a gun.

"I had never even seen a pistol before. I didn't know what to do, so I did what he said. He strapped me in here as soon as we arrived, and he pulled out some bottles of liquid, but he spoke to me first. He said that he wanted me to ruin my life. He said that I did not deserve the success I had had, and that the financial trouble would not be bothering me after today because everything else that happened would be worse."

She broke into sobs, and I held her hand. The others were moving around me, quietly searching the lab, but they had stopped to listen while she spoke. None of them moved then, like they were afraid that interrupting her anguish could break her. Finally, she stopped and looked up again.

"I'm sorry," she said. "I-"

"You don't have to apologise," I said, interrupting. "You said he spoke to you first. What did he do next?"

"Nothing. He saw something out of the window and ran behind me. I think he had been going to make me drink something from one of those bottles, or maybe inject it. He was turning it round and round in his hand."

"Then you're okay," I said.

"How do you know?" she asked, tears welling up again.

"I just do." I did my best to smile, and tried a question again. "What is your name?"

"Laura McRae," she said. I looked at Norton, and he nodded. She was in the yearbook then.

"Okay, Laura, and you said that he ran behind you?"

She nodded. Ashley and Harding had begun searching as she had said it the first time anyway, but as yet they had found nothing. I thanked her, and Norton and I joined the search while SCO-19 officers escorted her out.

As I looked around, it felt like something was out of place and, not being a scientist, it took me quite some time to figure out what. Then I saw it, and could not believe it had taken so long to hit me. There was no evidence anywhere of calculations or formulae. Whatever was going on here was either a true experiment with no discernible means of evaluating a result, or Evans knew precisely what he was doing without referring to notes of any kind. To be honest, both possibilities terrified me equally.

Norton in particular was distressed. He muttered to himself, and occasionally spoke out loud. He could sense Evans' presence, and confirmed that he had been in the lab not that long ago. Then my eye was caught by Ashley waving her hand and holding a finger to her lips. She pointed at a spot on the wall and mouthed: 'In here'. As quietly as we could, Harding, Norton and I walked over and peered at the wall.

She was right. There was the very faint outline of a panel in the wall. It was subtle and only really noticeable because of a slightly different organisation to the things around it. I realised what she must have seen, and my professional respect for her rose.

There was, in its own bizarre way, a certain method to the madness of the chemical apparatus. However, the line was broken near the opening in the wall. Things on the table had been slightly condensed so that ends of tubes were not over beakers and the 'production line' had been broken. I had ignored it as a pile of unused material, but I realised that it must have actually been hurriedly shoved out of the way. A couple of large heat mats were stacked against a unit a couple of feet from the panel, but they were at an awkward angle, and likely to fall at the slightest encouragement. It was not in keeping with the relatively meticulous nature of the lab.

There was also a very slight, almost invisible indentation in the wall itself, above the panel, that was the perfect size for a hand to slip under.

Harding nodded to Ashley and beckoned to the SCO-19 men to approach quietly and be ready. He gestured and mouthed to them that they should only fire on his command. They signalled understanding. He turned back to Ashley and raised his eyebrows. She nodded once and he returned the gesture. He reached forward and put his fingers under the panel. He counted to three and then pulled.

What happened next was almost a blur, and it took my mind a moment to process it. The panel clattered to the ground, revealing a very compact space - no more than two feet wide - hidden behind the wall. A second later, something flew out of the hole and the SCO-19 officers raised their weapons and snapped into a ready stance. Harding bellowed out to hold fire, and they looked at him waiting for orders. Meanwhile, my eyes caught up with the small missile just in time to see a glass test tube sail past Ashley's head and smash on a unit behind her, splashing her face and open mouth with liquid as it went by.

48

Everyone went silent for a second, surprised into inaction, despite our preparedness. I wondered whether to grab for my gas mask again, but no vapour seemed to be emitted by the liquid. Ashley shook her head, rubbing at the fluid with her shirt sleeves, trying to get the it off her face.

"God what is that?" she cried. "It smells awful. Ugh."

She was spluttering and choking and my heart was suddenly in my throat as I realised that she must have all but swallowed some of the liquid and she was fighting it. We all looked at each other, panicked expressions on our faces, and then a voice from behind us shouted, "Kill them."

Ashley's eyes glazed over for a moment, as if she were staring far beyond the walls of that hut, out of the wood, and into the great distance of space. Then they refocused, and her face took on the grim expression of a death mask. She backed away three paces to one of the units, picked up a pair of thin glass beakers and smashed them, spilling their liquid over herself, the unit and the floor. She adopted a kind of low fighting stance, holding broken glass in both hands and emitting a feral growl.

Guns were immediately trained on her, and more SCO-19 men burst in at the door. Windows were also smashed in, and gun barrels and helmeted heads appeared through them. The armed men were bellowing at Ashley to drop the bottles, and Harding was trying desperately to be heard over them - ordering them to hold their fire.

I thought I knew what he was reacting to. She had dropped her gun and not just opened fire on us. We might be able to take her down without firearms. I could not tell whether it was the moment in which Evans appeared to take control and she lost focus, or her own willpower resisting the effect that made her do what she did, but it was a start. Norton and I both took steps forward, hoping to catch her off balance and pin her before anything more drastic was required.

I was a couple of feet closer than Norton was, and she swung at me with a bottle. I ducked back, and felt the breeze across my nose as her arm swept inches above and in front of me. She swung again, with both arms this time, and I managed to catch the first on my elbow, but the next was too close behind it yet just far enough for her to adjust the angle, and the edge of the broken bottle slashed across my forearm. I cried out and spun round, clutching at the wound. Whatever had been in the bottle added to the pain, and I fell to my knees.

The world seemed to slow down as I heard the voices around me get louder and more high pitched. I could not make out words, but I could hear what sounded like a keening battle cry from behind me. Suddenly that too was blocked out by the deafening crack of a gunshot. Even with the windows smashed out, in the metal hut the sound echoed round and round, and my ears started ringing.

When I looked up, however, the scene was quite different. Harding had clearly grabbed the arm of the gunman – an SCO-19 trooper – while Norton had reached out his arms to stop other officers from discharging their weapons. They stood now with guns down, but ready. Everyone else had been completely disoriented by the shot, including Ashley. She was clutching at her head and her eyes had taken on a different madness. The bottles had fallen to the floor and smashed. I watched in horror as she fell to her knees and one of them crunched down into the mass of broken glass. She cried out in pain.

A thin man had tumbled from the bolt-hole in the wall. He was shouting out, but he did not appear to have been hit. He seemed to be more unsettled than most, and he was clawing at his ears shouting out, "I can't hear. I can't hear."

Gradually we all regained our senses, and got to our feet. Ashley was by then sobbing on the floor, and the SCO-19 medical officer ran to her and began treating her wounds. I could see the skin on her left hand blistering and bubbling, and I wondered aghast at what had been in the bottles. When I saw the medic look at the hand, I hovered nearby just in case I needed something as a result of the wound she had dealt me, but he said that he would get to me in a moment and pushed me back.

Instead, I turned my attention to the man on the floor. He was covered in dust and cobwebs, presumably from the bolt-hole, but there was no mistaking the curly hair or the thick glasses that he still wore, albeit with different frames.

Harding walked over and pulled out his gun. He held it pointing at the man's head and spoke with a venom I had never heard before in his voice.

"Wesley Evans, you are under arrest for the murder of Ben and Christine Wattler, the killing of Terence Foxwood's dog, the murder of Simon Jefferies, and the attempted murders of Victor Jefferies and the family of Samantha Jung. Not to mention assault and attempted murder of officers of the law."

I thought I was going to throw up when I realised that his last comment was referring to me.

49

The end of the raid was incredibly anti-climactic. The local and Metropolitan Police officers, together with SCO-19, were sent back to their respective stations. Evans was taken into custody by us, officially acting as representatives of the police force, but the MSCE had him now, and he was going to see a very different kind of justice system to the one I was familiar with. I had expected an uncomfortable feeling to rise in me at that moment but somehow, after what I had seen, it did not come.

Ashley was taken to hospital. The wound on her knee was stable, although they had to extract the remaining glass fragments, but the one on her hand was more serious, and she had clearly sustained chemical burns. They also needed to test her to find out what was in the vial Evans had thrown at her. That was the one that worried me.

The medic had been momentarily concerned about my wound as well, but he realised that the contents of the bottle that Ashley had cut me with was plain iodine. The wound not being deep enough to warrant stitches, not having cut a major blood vessel, and having been effectively cleaned by its very nature, he simply bandaged me up and went on his way with his unit.

Wesley Evans was still moaning that he could not hear, and he had shown no sign of understanding the words that Harding had spoken to him during the arrest, nor of any spoken by anyone since.

He seemed almost like a stereotypical madman, sitting on the chair he had been unceremoniously dumped on and talking to himself. He was muttering nonsense, as far as we could tell, and Harding had set up a small dictaphone to record everything he said, just in case he incriminated himself or confessed to any of the crimes.

Norton was outside. The undiluted 'scent' of Evans' skill had finally gotten the better of him. He said that it could probably be compared to a combination of rotten eggs, burnt milk and untreated sewage, before walking to the edge of the clearing where the vehicles had been brought up. Not for the first time, I wondered exactly what he did sense with his own skill, and I was quite glad I did not know at that moment.

Harding was talking to the MI-5 agents in the corner of the room, away from me. They looked animated in their discussion, and it seemed to me that MI-5 was attempting to claim custody of Evans, but Harding was having none of it. Evidently having seen the altercation from outside, where he had been waiting by one of the MSCE vehicles, Detective Chief Superintendent Kwaku walked in, his face curled into the expressive equivalent of a snarl.

He flashed a police badge on entry, but when he got close I saw him draw out another one which I presumed to be some kind of high-level MSCE identification. Whatever it was, it had the desired effect, and the MI-5 officers backed away and left, though their faces expressed their displeasure.

Kwaku turned around and beckoned me over.

"We can take the suspect back to the MSCE office now," he said to Harding and me.

"Is he secure?" asked Harding.

"He is. Norton has confirmed the nature of his ability, now that he has been in close proximity to Evans." I gathered that the explanation was for my benefit. "Evans has an ability in manipulation of chemicals within his own body, and an extremely intelligent mind when it comes to chemistry. We need to study his creation further, but I believe that he is now harmless. The ability requires the external formula to be a threat, it would seem, and the one is apparently inert without the other."

"Nevertheless, appropriate precautions will be taken. You and Soames will have the honours, along with Barrett and McCabe. Norton cannot stand being near him, and will ride with me."

"Very well," said Harding. "I look forward to grilling this guy. What's wrong with him though? Why is he muttering and ignoring us?"

"His file says that he has extremely sensitive hearing. I did not place much importance on that earlier, but it seems that the massive sonic effect of the gunshot has disoriented him and made him temporarily unable to hear. It is difficult to say whether his hearing will recover in due course, but we shall see."

"What happens now?" I asked.

"Come with me and see," said Harding.

We left the hut, dragging Evans with us. We moved to the largest MSCE vehicle, a big, unmarked four-by-four flanked by the two men I recognised as having burst into my home with Harding the night I was recruited. These must be Barrett and McCabe. They opened the door as we approached.

The interior was that of a regular vehicle, with the exception of the middle seat in the back. The arms looked as though they stayed permanently down and could not retract into the seat back. Straps ran over them and around the foot well, as well as one on the headrest. Barrett and McCabe pushed Evans into the chair and strapped him in. It looked like some kind of torture device, and I wondered fleetingly about the legality, but given the nature of some of the suspects they likely brought in, it seemed a necessary measure.

Harding did not even bother holding Evans at gunpoint while he was strapped in. Evans was now mute and seemingly still deaf. He was moving his lips, but no sound was coming out. He looked back once at the lab as he was pushed into the car, but that was the only movement he made other than those encouraged by the guards. Once he was in, Harding looked at me.

"Fancy having a chat with Mr Wesley Evans in a private interview room where he cannot do any harm?"

I rather found that I did.

50

The interview room at the headquarters of the Metropolitan Special Circumstance Executive was nicknamed The Chamber, and its appearance was as ominous as that name suggested. It was entirely made of stone and painted black. The door had no inside handle, and was opened by a buzzer in the observation room, which nestled behind a two-way mirror set into the wall.

The interview room itself had two cameras - one was overtly placed in the corner of the room, but there was another miniature one embedded into a stone block in the wall in case a suspect agreed to talk without observation. With the kind of people this room held, there was simply no way the MSCE could not record their statements. Objections to this breach of confidence should have screamed inside my mind, but they hovered at the back as I thought about the man I was going to speak to in there.

Wesley Evans was not going to be a problem. The whole journey back, he sat looking glum in the prisoner's seat of the car. He did not complain or resist, but looked defeated. If I had not known everything that he had done, I might have felt sad for him. As it was, the expression only made me feel greater contempt. I shuddered to think about what he felt he had not accomplished.

On arrival at headquarters, Evans was immediately put into The Chamber. Harding, Norton and I went to the observation room and watched him for a couple of minutes to see his reaction, but there was none. He sat there as glumly as he had in the car.

"You observing this time, Norton?" asked Harding.

"Yes, please. I don't want to be in that room any longer than I need to be."

"Okay. Soames, you're with me."

I nodded. "What's the play?"

"Talk to him. Nothing more than that. I don't actually think that he is going to give us much grief. However, I feel that we may need to bring a tablet to type on, unless he knows sign-language."

"He doesn't. I tried it already," said Norton.

"You do?" Harding sounded surprised.

"One of my family was born deaf," Norton replied. His tone suggested that it was a sore point, and he turned away as he said it. I dragged Harding away before he could make the situation awkward. We collected a tablet from the tech office and entered The Chamber.

Evans made no indication that our arrival had registered with him. He stared at the table, motionless but for a slight twitch in his right hand. I sat down in front of him, and he finally looked up, but showed no other expression.

"Can you hear us yet, Wesley?" I asked.

He made no response. Harding circled around behind him and suddenly clapped his hands loudly right behind Evans' head. He did not so much as blink. I shook my head at Harding and he came and sat beside me. He took the tablet and typed out: *We will ask questions on this and you will answer. Understand? I will repeat everything out loud for the recording.*

Evans nodded. "Yes." He shouted the word, evidently not realising how loudly he was speaking. Harding typed *Quieter.* Evans nodded again.

"Do you admit your culpability in the deaths of Ben Wattler, Christine Wattler and Simon Jefferies, along with the killing of Terence Foxwood's dog and the attempted murders of Victor Jefferies and the family of Samantha Jung?" Harding asked. His fingers moved dextrously over the keyboard while Evans watched them impassively.

When Harding had finished, Evans stared at the screen for a moment. It was as though he was weighing in his mind precisely how to answer the question. He was evidently a broken man, but I got the sense that the break had begun to occur before our intervention.

"Yes," he said, finally. His voice was slightly more moderated, although still loud. He spoke very deliberately, as though he had to feel the word to be sure he was saying the right thing.

"Why?" asked Harding.

"You would not understand," replied Evans.

"Try me." The tablet conveyed no emotion, but Harding's expression was black.

"I did not directly wish to hurt Christine or Victor. I only wanted to hurt Ben and Simon and Terry and Samantha." He spoke like a child would, listing everything out and tallying off on his fingers. His mind was clearly still a bit befuddled from the sonic assault. "I wanted to hurt Marshall and Laura and Faith too."

I remembered seeing those names in the yearbook, though I could not bring Marshall's face to mind. Obviously Laura was Laura MacRae.

"What did they do to deserve that?" asked Harding.

Evans sat back and sighed. "They hurt me. They ruined my life. I did not want to hurt them back necessarily, but I wanted to ruin their lives. I was a genius at school. I had great potential at science, but they did not respect me. I did not understand at the time that there was something different about me, and they just saw someone who they thought was trying to show off. I think the difference is what made me smart. They didn't understand that. They made my life a complete misery. I was beaten up, insulted and they sabotaged my work at every opportunity."

"It grew so bad that I was unable to come and go from school without my mother. I started arriving late and leaving as soon as classes were over so that I could get away from them, but they could still get at me during the day. It was meant to be a good school, but it was not good to me. The only place I was safe was in the science labs. They were too afraid of breaking something dangerous to follow me in there."

"I became agoraphobic and anti-social. I could deal with the agoraphobia as long as there were no people nearby, which is why I worked in the woods. I should have been a master scientist, but instead I was confined within my own head, only able to perform experiments at home."

"I discovered my ability to manipulate chemicals by accident, although it probably saved Simon Jefferies from serious trouble, when he was too young to know better. At school, he swapped out my water for hydrochloric acid. I realised what it was before I swallowed and was naturally terrified, but somehow my saliva changed the composition so that it was harmless. I do not know how it works to this day - I have experimented on myself for years - but it does. I could have turned him in I suppose, but I realised that I had something I could use against him when I chose to do so - and all the others as well. Marshall was the worst, and I was saving him for last. I would have enjoyed getting at him."

"Through my experiments, I came across a formula that I could modify which would allow me to implant a suggestion into a subject's mind. It never worked the same way every time because every person is different. It was a completely harmless solution until it merged with a subject's saliva, at which point they would take the first command they heard from me to be the driving force in their lives."

"My first tests were relatively benign. I forcibly overcame my agoraphobia and moved to Marshall's Watch Farm - the irony of the name amused me. I made people do things like run round their gardens ten times or something crazy like that. They never remembered what had happened afterwards, and I realised that I had the perfect weapon. I could force those who had ruined my life years before to ruin their own lives."

"People have weaknesses, you know. I got them all to come to me by revealing secrets about them that I had hoarded up. I said I simply wanted to talk, and that I would say nothing of the titbit of their lives after that. Or maybe that I could help them with their problem. Or make them feel better. I would even do that, because then my ruination would be much more complete. Terence came first, and then Ben and Simon. Samantha and Laura were the last, and I was going to see Faith tomorrow. I told them I just wanted an apology for their treatment of me. Terry and Simon apologised, although they did not mean it. Samantha said she did not want to and Ben refused. Laura just cried."

"It did not matter by then. I had spiked their drinks with the formula, and I told them to ruin their lives. I did not expect the means to be quite so violent, but I was impressed with how diligently they tried to carry out their tasks. Ben's dose was higher than the rest because he annoyed me. Simon's failed because of something in his biology, I guess - I never really understood biology. I don't know what happened with Samantha. I am just sorry that my work remains unfinished."

With that, Evans closed his mouth and looked down at the table again. Harding and I sat staring at him. We shared a glance at one point. Never in my life had I seen an interrogation subject fold so completely. His rational mind was obviously too aware of the situation, and had given up fighting. He was spent and had destroyed himself in the process of attempting to exact his terrible retribution. He sagged in the chair even as we watched. Nevertheless, there were two more questions we had to ask, and Harding typed them out on the tablet and forced it under Evans' nose.

Is that what you threw at our friend?
Evans nodded.

How long do the effects of the formula last if the subject does not carry out your command?

He looked up once more and appeared genuinely pained. I realised before he spoke that his comment about his work remaining unfinished referred not just to his intended victims, but to his perfection of his drug. I knew what he was going to say before he said it, and I stared into those eyes as he spoke.

"I don't know."

51

I think, in some ways, I was still stunned by everything I had learned, and I found myself unable to speak out against and question the somewhat oppressive nature of the MSCE. I knew from experience what living with reservations could do, but I did it anyway.

I wrote my paperwork out longhand, of course. I had picked out a simple but efficient pen from the selection I had been offered, and I was a little surprised by how quickly I regained my flowing handwriting – I had never been a neat writer, but my work had always been legible. Two paragraphs into my report, I screwed up the piece of paper and started again, and this time the letters were neat from the outset.

There was something reassuring in the feel of the pen as well. The smooth, black-lacquered cylinder brought back a memory of my father, and I stopped writing momentarily to indulge my nostalgia.

I had been nine, I think, maybe ten. My mother had driven me home from school on the last day of the year. I was excited for eight weeks of no work besides my house chores. Dad had been in his study when we got to the house, and I had stood in the door for a moment, watching him before I went in to what he referred to as his sanctuary.

I think that it was the first time I had really looked at my father. He was an old man in my mind, but only because he was fifty-something. He certainly did not look it. He had been writing a letter, and had his head bent low over his desk, his left cheek dimpled as he chewed on it. It was something he did when he was thinking. I tried it once, and all I did was hurt my cheek.

He had looked so serene in that moment. His study had been a thing of beauty, with an orange glow thrown by the fabric cover of a desk lamp. The rest of the house was functional, but the study was another world – his sanctuary; his world; his escape from the real one.

He had noticed me a moment later, and the picture had broken as his eyes lit up and he rushed over and lifted me up, talking about the holiday we were going to go on, and the camping trip he wanted to take with me up north.

I remembered that same doorway three years later. The study had taken on a dull colour as dust shrouded the surfaces, the books, and the rug on the floor. His pen still stood in its holder on the side of his desk. I had wished for him to walk past me, pick that pen up, and begin writing another letter, but he never would again.

I walked over to the desk myself. The pen was dusty. I picked it up, blew the dust off, and coughed as I disturbed the layer on the desk as well. The pen was dark brown with a gold nib, and near the top it was engraved with the letters TDS. Thomas Dean Soames.

I still had the pen in a drawer at home. I had got it out the day Kwaku had offered me a pen, but I could not bring myself to write with it. I did not even know if it still worked. I had put it back, and picked something completely different. Function over form, as the rest of the house had been. Dad's pen belonged in his other world.

There was one other thing I had taken from that room, and I thought about that now, as I held my writing hand over the sheet of paper. I had found it on the desk inside one of the small drawers set into the back. It was a small sheet of thick, ornate paper – not even A6-size – with my father's neat, formal handwriting on it.

It said: *Believe in yourself, for only then can others see you for who you truly are.*

I looked at the half-written report in front of me, complete up to our meeting with Victor Jefferies, and I wondered how others could know who I truly was when I did not even know myself.

52

The next stage of Evans' incarceration took place a couple of days later, and was actually not as different as I had expected from the trials I had attended as a police officer, with a couple of fairly obvious exceptions.

As a result of the extraordinary nature of the case, it was obvious that the general public could not be allowed to learn of Evans' power. One of the objectives of the MSCE was to hide the existence of these people and thus prevent the panic that would undoubtedly ensue if they were uncovered. How could anyone feel safe knowing that any person they passed in the street might be able to control their mind, change their identity or know their innermost secrets?

The jury for the trial was made up of MSCE members who had not taken part in the investigation, plus two MI-5 liaison agents. I remembered the comment Kwaku had made about the Secret Service acting as a watchdog over our activities. Harding was the prosecuting officer and Evans had to man his own defence, although a trained legal officer was on hand to advise him. However, in this case, there was no question of his guilt. Norton confirmed that the skill scent matched that of Evans, and Evans' own recorded admission of guilt was sufficient for the jury to convict him.

A file was created for Subject 084582. Wesley Evans became that number to the MSCE, and his name was committed within the file. He was listed as a moderate- to high-risk subject, due to the comparatively limited scope of his power, but the malicious intent with which he had used it. He was sentenced to life imprisonment, without parole. A letter would be sent to his family explaining that he had been lost in a plane crash over the Pacific Ocean, and he would disappear completely. The Metropolitan Special Circumstance Executive did not shrink from severe punitive measures when it came to murder.

There were a few doors in the Penthouse that I had not been through yet, but one that I had never even seen before. A panel in the wall of the main office was slid open and Kwaku, as well as Harding and I, had to apply our thumbs and forefingers to a biometric scanner. Thus one of the chief officers of the MSCE, together with the two arresting officers, were logged as having opened the door to the prison cells.

Kwaku explained that it was necessary for me to see what was down there, and I followed him in, Harding bringing Evans along behind us. We rode an elevator down still further under the ground, and the door finally opened to the cells.

At first, I was completely unsure of what I was looking at. Rows and rows of black cylinders lined the walls and the floor of the gigantic cavern into which the elevator opened. They were some five feet across and seven feet tall, and seemed to have cables feeding into them around their lowest circumference and into the very top. We walked past them, but although they appeared to be made of glass or plastic, it was completely opaque, and I could not begin to guess at what was inside them.

However, we stopped at one and Kwaku made us all enter our prints again, and then pressed Evans' thumb to the lock. The cylinder slid open and the glass became transparent. Kwaku removed Evans' handcuffs and gestured for him to enter the pod. It appeared to be bare metal for the most part, with a padded human outline in it. As Evans stepped in, lasers appeared and moved around him, apparently scanning his form. The housing shifted and increased or decreased dimensions until it fit Evans perfectly. Then the sliding cover closed, but remained see-through.

I watched, feeling the entire gamut of emotions, as the chamber filled with what looked like gas, and I realised what I was seeing.

"It's a cryogenic chamber," said Kwaku. "MSCE prisoners with a classification above low-risk who are sentenced to life imprisonment are sealed in here. The technology we are using here is completely covert, and very few people know of its existence. It is the only way we are able to contain the threat that these people present."

"But that's barbaric," I said.

"Perhaps. But consider what some of these people can do."

We began to walk out, and he spoke as we went, pointing to the canisters as he did so.

"Subject 048821, Matthias Green. With a word and a particular tone of voice, he can give you such waking nightmares that you lose your mind, but also suffered those same nightmares himself. He went mad, committed twenty-seven people to insane asylums and killed eight more before we caught him. He had been running from his own mind, and held no remorse for his actions."

"Subject 099530, Severine Gresset. She can access and edit any piece of technology's data storage simply by touching it. She stole almost half a billion pounds sterling and three billion Euros before we managed to stop her, not to mention assuming multiple identities, including that of a member of the United Nations. Her actions opened a backdoor into a foreign government database on English soil, and five of that government's agents were killed as a result."

"Subject 022100, Leon Campbell. He is incapable of touching anything living without killing it instantly. We went to arrest him after he killed both his parents, his four-year-old sister, the babysitter, an ambulance paramedic and two policemen - not to mention the entire flora and most of the fauna in his parents' garden. He remanded himself into our custody as soon as he understood who we were."

"Four-year-old sister," I interruped. "How old is he?"

"He was fourteen years and six days old when he was frozen. We kept him in a non-cryogenic cell for a year while we fought over what to do with him. I did not want him to enter cryogenics until he was old enough to understand the full scope of his decision. However, he killed an MSCE agent who tripped over in his cell while bringing him food. At the time, the MSCE was rather more mercenary than we are now, and that sealed his fate."

I had no idea what I thought about that. I had assumed that all of the hits had landed when it came to the organisation, but this was the biggest one yet.

"Take your time, Soames. We normally take this all a lot slower with a new recruit, but the nature of your entrance to the Executive was far more abrupt than many. Evans' confession saved us from a lot of the legal debates that can surround these situations. It may take you a while to decide how to process all this, but you will. I know people, and I choose people carefully."

We exited the cells and the hidden door sealed behind us. Even so, I would carry those memories with me for the rest of my life, whether I wished to or not.

"Come and see me when you're ready," said Kwaku, and walked back to his office.

I wondered if I would ever be ready.

53

I went to visit Ashley in hospital to see how she was. I bumped into Barrett on his way out who said that she seemed to be in good spirits, although she was heavily sedated, and it was possible that the drugs explained her mood. The burns on her hand had been caused by concentrated phosphoric acid. Her hand would likely never fully recover, but they had managed to stop any further damage from occurring.

Her knee was only a flesh wound and would recover quickly, though sixteen fragments of glass had been removed from it. She had shaken off the effects of Evans' formula much more quickly than could have been expected, and for that I was enormously relieved.

I entered the room with some trepidation, but she greeted me with a drugged smile.

"Hey," she said.

"Hey to you too," I replied.

"I'm sorry I don't look as good as usual."

"You look fine. I'm glad to find you back to normal."

"I'm sorry I hurt you."

"It's nothing. Honestly. You know you hit me with an iodine bottle? I don't think I've ever had such a clean cut."

She tried to laugh, but it came out as a rasping sound, and her breathing rate increased to compensate.

"Ow. My stomach hurts," she said.

"Are you okay?"

"It's fine. They gave me an emetic to get rid of Evans' chemicals."

"Charming." I grinned.

"Don't worry, sexy. I'll be back at you soon."

She had been blinking slower and slower and finally she closed her eyes and fell asleep. I was glad that she had her sense of humour back, but I was very unsure about her attempts at flirting, however drug-induced they might have been. Physically, she was the woman of my dreams, but she was associated with something that I did not fully understand or condone, and I did not know if I would ever be able to trust her. At the thought of trust, Emily's face flashed into my mind, and I wondered what I could ever tell her to explain the haunted look I was sure I would be wearing for some time to come.

I had used the phrase 'life-changing moment' a couple of times to describe events in my life, but I had never truly appreciated its significance. Walking out of that hospital, I suddenly got exactly what it meant. My best friend wanted an explanation that I did not even have for myself. If I did have it, I could never give it to him. My own mind had been raped with the knowledge that had been put into it over the last few days, and I felt physically sick just thinking about some of it. No matter what I did, I could never go back to the way things had been before.

Even worse, I did not know what I felt about the cryogenic stasis. Putting Evans in there had felt like a step too far for me at the time, but I did not doubt that it was the safest method of containment for some of the inhabitants of that black prison. I was also worried about the fact that someone like Creeker was free. Regardless of the fact that he had to be close enough to initiate contact, if he caught you unawares, you would have absolutely no idea that something was wrong.

I passed through the main doors to the hospital and was surprised to see Norton leaning against a blue Toyota Yaris. He was also wearing black jeans and a long-sleeved t-shirt. It seemed very strange to see him looking remotely casual.

"Yours?" I asked, nodding to the car.

"Yep," he said. "This is me when I'm not Sniffer."

I smiled, wearily. He pressed the unlock button on his keys. "Hop in."

I climbed into the passenger seat of the car and suddenly felt safe. I did not know what it was about Norton but, somehow, despite his allegiances, I felt like I could trust him. He knew far more than I did about the Metropolitan Special Circumstance Executive, and yet it was obvious that he was very concerned about the existence of his own kind, and it was no secret that he was dedicated to upholding justice for everyone. That made him different, in my mind. Someone like Creeker did not let his motivations show so easily and I had no idea what drove him. I had not spent enough time with him to decipher the man behind the codename, and I was not sure I wanted to.

Then I realised that I had used the phrase 'his own kind'. Even though it had been in my mind, that made me feel guilty, as I realised that I could be susceptible to the very prejudice the organisation was worried about.

Norton started the engine and pulled out of the parking lot.

"How are you?" he asked.

I snorted. "Honestly, I have absolutely no idea whatsoever."

"I'm not surprised. This was very hard on you. At least some people have it easier or slower. In an ideal world, someone would come in on a slow-burn, low-risk case, and in that situation everything would be drip-fed. Having it rammed down your throat like it was was a very cruel thing to do. But you do understand that Kwaku had no choice?"

Somehow, hearing Norton say that to me allowed my mind to process it. "Yes," I said. "And to be honest, it is not the whole that has me bothered now. Having seen what I have seen, I accept that such people are out there. It is the aftermath that concerns me. Does that make me a bad, what are we, agent? Officer?"

"No. It makes you human. In all honesty, I would be genuinely worried if you were happy with it all. It is a dark thing that we do, and your conscience is the only thing that keeps you from falling into a very bad place. If you did not think about it, I would not offer you the hand of friendship. Maybe that is harsh, but there it is."

"Thank you, Norton. That actually means a lot."

"Did you notice something about Kwaku in the prison? He makes a point of demonstrating it to every recruit."

"What?"

"He remembers the name of every single prisoner in that place. He has signed in enough in his time, and he makes it his mission to know who is in there, so that they are not just forgotten and left to rot."

I had not considered that at the time, but there was something in what Norton said, and it made me feel better. Kwaku had proved to me that he too was human, and that he carried a very great weight on his shoulders. Now that we were not in the oppressive environs of the cells, I could see that he did not take his job lightly. That, at least, gave me some encouragement.

"You know, I hadn't noticed that," I said. "Thank you for pointing it out to me."

"My pleasure."

I considered what he had said for a moment, and let it really sink in. I had no idea what I thought of the Executive, but at least Kwaku was not as bad as I had thought him not so long before. I looked up and realised that I was unsure of where we were.

"Where are we going?" I asked.

"The Last Glass," replied Norton. "I thought you might want a drink."

"Like you would not believe," I said, and then had a thought, injecting an edge of fear into my voice. "What if Harry is there? I'm not ready to deal with him yet."

Norton stopped me. "We go somewhere else," he said.

I would have to face Harry sooner or later; Emily, too. Now, however, there were other battles to be fought. Maybe there were things out there that I did not understand. Maybe everything that

I had stood for had been torn out from under my feet in the past week. Maybe there were things I had participated in that I had to reconcile with my own morals.

Maybe I was, in fact, questioning precisely what my reality was at that moment in time.

Still, one thing I could always be sure of was the feel of a cold beer glass.